Simak...
Simak...
Simak...

three stories three times as weird by one of the master writers of this, or any, world

WORLDS WITHOUT END

by Clifford D. Simak

BELMONT BOOKS • NEW YORK CITY

WORLDS WITHOUT END

A BELMONT BOOK

Published by
Belmont Productions, Inc.
66 Leonard Street, New York, N. Y. 10013

cover painting by Richard Powers

Contents

WORLDS WITHOUT END

I

SHE DID NOT look like the kind of person who would want to take the Dream. Although, Norman Blaine reflected, one could never tell.

He wrote the name she had given him down on the scratch pad, instead of putting it on the application blank, he wrote it slowly, deliberately, to give himself time to think, for there was something here that was puzzling.

Lucinda Silone.

Peculiar name, he thought. Not like a real name. More like a stage name taken to cover up plain Susan Brown, or ordinary Betty Smith, or some other common run of name.

He wrote it slowly so that he could think, but he couldn't think too well. There were too many other things cluttering up his brain: The shakeup rumor that had whispered its way for days back and forth within the Center, his own connection with that rumor, and the advice that had been given him—there was something funny about the job. The advice was: don't trust Farris (as if he needed that advice!)—look it over well if it is offered you. It was all kindly-meant advice, but not very helpful.

And there was the lapel-clinging Buttonholer who had caught him in the parking lot that morning and had clung onto him when he tried to push him off; there was Harriet Marsh, with whom he had a date this very night.

Now, finally, this woman across the desk from him.

Although it was foolish, Blaine told himself—to think a thing like that, to tie her up with all the other thoughts that were bumping together like driftwood in his brain. For there could be no connection—there simply couldn't be.

7

She was Lucinda Silone, she'd said. Something about
the name and something, as well, about the way she said
it—the little lilting tones meant consciously to give it
grace and make it sparkle—set tiny alarm bells ringing
in his brain.

"You're with Entertainment." He said it casually, very
much off-hand; this was a trick question and one that
must be rightly put.

"Why, no," she replied, "I'm not."

Listening to the way she said it, Blaine could find nothing wrong. Her voice held a touch of fluttery happiness
that betrayed pleasure at his thinking she must be Entertainment. And that was just as it should be. It was exactly
the way that most of the others answered—flattered at the
implication that they belonged to the fabulous Entertainment guild.

He gave her her money's worth. "I would have guessed
you were."

He looked directly at Lucinda Silone, watching the expression on her face, but seeing all the other good points,
too. "We get good at judging people here," he said. "We
aren't often wrong."

She didn't wince. There was no reaction—no start of
guilt, no flutter of confusion.

Her hair was honey color, her eyes were china blue, and
her skin so milky white that one looked a second time to
make sure that it was real.

We don't get many like this one, thought Blaine. *The
old and sick and the disappointed. The desperate ones
and those who know frustration.*

"You're mistaken, Mr. Blaine," she said. "I am Education."

He wrote *Education* on the scratch pad, and said, "It
may have been the name. It's a very good name. Easy to
say. Musical. It would go well on the stage."

He looked up from the pad and said, smiling—making
himself smile against the inexplicable tension that was
rising in him: "Although it was not the name alone; I am
sure of that."

She didn't smile and he wondered swiftly if he had
been awkward. He snapped the words he'd said in quick
review across his mind and decided that he'd not been

awkward. When you were director of Fabrication, you were not an awkward man. You knew how to handle people; you had to know how to handle them. And you knew, as well, how to handle yourself—how to make your face say one thing while your mind might be thinking something else.

No, his words had been a compliment, and not too badly put. She should have smiled. That she had failed to smile might mean something—or it mightn't mean a thing, except that she was clever. Norman Blaine had no doubt that Lucinda Silone was clever, and as cool a customer as he had ever seen.

Although coolness in itself was not too unusual. You got the cool ones, too—the cool and calculating—the ones who had figured it all out well ahead of time and knew what they were doing. And there were others, too, who had cut off all retreat behind them.

"You wish a Sleep," he said.

She nodded.

"And a Dream?"

"And a Dream," she said.

"You've thought it out quite thoroughly, I suppose. You wouldn't come, of course, if you had any doubts."

"I've thought it through," she told him, "and I have no doubts."

"You still have time. You'll have time to change your mind up to the final moment. We're most anxious that you get that fact fixed firmly in your mind."

"I'll not change my mind," she said.

"We still prefer to assume you may. We do not try to change your mind, but we insist upon complete understanding upon your part that a change is possible. You are under no obligation to us. No matter how far we've gone, there still is no obligation. The Dream may have been fabricated and processed; you may have paid your fee; you may already have entered the receptacle—there's still time to change your mind. The Dream will then be destroyed, your fee will be returned, and the record will be expunged. So far as we are then concerned, we will have never seen you."

"I quite understand," she said.

He nodded quietly. "We'll proceed on that understanding."

He picked up his pencil and wrote her name and classification on the application blank. "Age?"

"Twenty nine."

"Married?"

"No."

"Children?"

"None."

"Nearest of kin?"

"An aunt."

"Name?"

She gave him the name and he wrote it down, with address, age and classification of the aunt.

"Any others?"

"None at all."

"Your parents?"

Her parents had been dead for years, she said; she was an only child. She gave her parents' names, their classifications, their ages at the time of death, their last place of residence, their place of burial.

"You'll check on all of this?" she asked.

"We check on everything."

Here was the place where most of the applicants—even those who had nothing in their life to hide—would show some nervousness, would frantically start checking back along their memories to unearth some possible, long-forgotten incident which might turn up in the course of investigation to embarrass or impede them.

Lucinda Silone was not nervous; she sat there, waiting for the other questions.

Norman Blaine asked them: The number of her guild, her card number, her immediate superior, last medical exam, physical or psychic defects or ailments—all the other trivia which went into the details of daily life.

Finally he was finished and laid the pencil down. "Still no doubts?"

She shook her head.

"I keep harking back to that," said Blaine, "to make absolutely certain we have a willing client; otherwise we have no legal status. But aside from that, there is the matter of ethics . . ."

"I understand," she said, "that you are very ethical."

It might have been mockery; if so, it was very clever mockery. He tried to decide if it were or not, but he wasn't sure.

He let it drop. "We have to be," he told her. "Here is a setup which, to survive, must be based on the highest code of ethics. You give your body into our hands for our safekeeping over a number of years. What is more, you give your mind over to us, to a lesser extent. We gain much intimate knowledge of your life in the course of our work with you. To continue in the job we're doing, we must enjoy the complete confidence not only of our clients, but of the general public. The slightest breath of scandal..."

"There has never been a scandal?"

"In the early days, there were a few. They've been forgotten now, or we hope they have. It was those early scandals which made our guild realize how important it was that we keep ourselves free of any professional taint. A scandal in any of the other guilds is no more than a legal matter which can be adjudicated in the courts and then forgiven and forgotten. But with us there'd be no forgiving or forgetting; we'd never live it down."

Sitting there, Norman Blaine thought of his pride in the work he did—a bright and shining pride, a comfortable and contented pride in a job well done. And this feeling was not confined to he himself alone, but was held by everyone at Center. They might be flippant when they talked among themselves, but the pride was there, hidden deep beneath the flippancy and the workaday approach.

"You almost sound," she said, "like a dedicated people."

Mockery again, he wondered. Or was it flattery to match his own. He smiled a little at it. "Not dedicated," he said. "At least, we never think of ourselves as dedicated."

And that was not quite right, he knew, for there were times when every one of them must have thought of themselves as dedicated. It was not a thing, of course, that one could say aloud—but the thought was there.

It was a strange situation, he thought—the pride of work, the fierce loyalty to the guild itself, and, then, the cutthroat competition, and the vicious Center politics which existed in the midst of that pride and loyalty.

Take Roemer for example. Roemer, who after years of work, was on his way out. That had been the talk for days —the open secret which had been whispered through the Center. Farris had something to do with it, Lew Giesey was invovled in some way, and there were others who were mentioned. Blaine himself, for example, had been mentioned as one of the men who might be chosen to step up into Roemer's position. Thank goodness, he had steered clear of Center politics all these years. There was too much headache in Center politics. Norman Blaine's work had been enough for him.

Although it would be fine, he thought, if he were picked to take over Roemer's job. It was higher up the ladder; the pay was better; and maybe if he got more money he could talk Harriet into giving up her newspaper job and . . .

He pulled himself back to the job at hand.

"There are certain considerations which you should take into account," he told the woman across the desk. "You should realize all the implications of what your decision means before you go ahead. You must realize that once you go to sleep, you will awaken in a culture different than your own. The planets will not stand still while you sleep; they will advance—or at least we hope they will. Much will be different. Styles will change, in clothing and in manners. Thought and speech and per-spective—all will change. You will awaken an alien in a world that has left you far behind; you will be old fashioned.

There will be public issues of which there now is not the faintest inkling. Governments may have evolved, and customs will be different. What is illegal today may have become quite acceptable; what is acceptable and legal to-day may have become outrageous or illegal then. Your friends will all be dead . . ."

"I have no friends," Lucinda Silone said.

He disregarded her and went on: "What I am trying to impress upon you is that once you wake you cannot step from here straight back into the world, for it will be your world no longer. Your world will have died many years before; you will have to be readjusted, will have to take a course in reorientation. In certain instances, depending upon the awakened person to some extent, to the cultural changes to an even greater extent, this matter of reorientation may take quite some time. For we must give you not only the facts of the changes which have occurred while you were asleep—we must gain your acceptance of those changes. Until you have readjusted not only your data, but your culture as well, we cannot let you go. To live a normal life in that world in which you wake you must accept it as if you had been born into it—you must become, in fact, part of it. And that must often be a long and painful process."

"I realize all that," she said; "I'm ready to abide by all the conditions you lay down."

She had not hesitated once. Lucinda Silone had shown no regret or nervousness. She was as cool and calm as when she'd walked into the office.

"Now," Blaine said, "the reason."

"The reason?"

"The reason why you wish to take the Sleep; we must know."

"You'll investigate that, too?"

"We shall; we must be sure, you see. There are many reasons—many more than you'd think there'd be."

He kept on talking, to give her a chance to steel herself and tell him the reason. More often than not this was the hardest thing of all that a client faced. "There are those," he said, "who take the Sleep because they have a disease which at the moment is incurable. They do not contract for a Sleep of any specified length, but only till the day when a cure has been discovered.

"Then there are those who wish to wait out the time against the return of a loved one who is traveling to the stars—waiting out on Earth the subjective time of the faster-than-light flights. And there are those who wish to sleep out an investment which they are sure, given time, will make them a fortune. Usually we try to talk them out of it; we call in our economists, who try to show them . . ."

She interrupted him. "Would ennui be enough?" she asked. "Just simple ennui?"

He wrote *ennui* for the reason and shoved the application to one side. "You can sign it later."

"I can sign it now."

"We'd prefer you wait a little."

Blaine fiddled with the pencil, trying to think it out—wondering why this client should disturb him so. Lucinda Silone was wrong and he couldn't place the wrongness; yet, he knew he should be able to, for he met all sorts of clients.

"If you wish," he said, "we could discuss the Dream. Usually we don't but . . ."

"Let's discuss it," she said.

"A Dream is not necessary," he told her. "There are those who take the Sleep without one. I don't wish to appear to be arguing against a Dream; in many cases it appears to me to be preferable. You would not be conscious of the time—an hour or a century is no longer than a second. You go to sleep; then you wake, and it is as if there had been no time at all . . ."

"I want a Dream," she said.

"In that case, we are glad to serve you. Have you thought what kind?"

"A friendly dream. A restful one and friendly."

"No excitement? No adventure?"

"Some; perhaps, it might get monotonous otherwise. But genteel, if you please."

"A polite society, perhaps," suggested Blaine. "Let's say, one much concerned with manners."

"And no competition, if you can manage it; no rushing about to beat out someone else."

"An old, established home," continued Blaine. "Good position in the community, high family traditions; sufficient income to banish money worries."

"It sounds a bit archaic."

"It's the kind of Dream you asked for."

"Of course," she said. "What am I thinking of? It will be lovely. It's the sort of thing, the sort . . ." she laughed. "The sort of thing you dream of."

He laughed with her.

"You like it? We can change it, bring it up to date."

"Don't you dare, it's just what I want."

"You'll want to be young, I suppose, younger than twenty-nine—sixteen or seventeen."

She nodded.

"And pretty, of course, you would be beautiful despite anything we did."

She did not answer.

"Plenty of admirers," he said. "We could put in lots of them."

She nodded.

"Sexual adventures?"

" A few, don't overdo it, though."

"We'll keep it dignified," he promised. "You'll have no regrets; we'll give you a Dream you'll need not be ashamed of—one you can look back upon with a lot of happiness. There naturally will have to be some disappointments, a few heart-aches; happiness can't run on forever without getting stale. There must be something, even in a Dream, upon which you can establish comparative values."

"I'll leave that all to you."

"All right, then, we'll get to work on it. Could you come back, say in three days' time? We'll have it roughed out then and we can go over it together. It may take half a dozen—well, let us call them fittings, before we have what you want."

Lucinda Silone rose and held out her hand. Her clasp was firm and friendly. "I'll stop at the cashier's and pay the fee," she said. "And thanks, so very much."

"There's no need to pay the fee this soon."

"I'll feel better when I do."

Norman Blaine watched her go, then sat back down again. The intercom buzzed. "Yes, Irma."

His secretary said, "Harriet called. You were with the client, and couldn't be disturbed; she left a message."

"What did she want?"

"Just to let you know she can't have dinner with you tonight. She said something about an assignment, some big bug from Centauri."

He said: "Irma, let me give you a tip. Never fall in love with Communications. You can't depend on them."

"You keep forgetting, Mr. Blaine; I married Transportation."

"So I do," said Blaine.

"George and Herb are out here waiting. They've been slapping one another on the back and rolling on the floor. Take them off my hands before I go stark raving."

"Send them in," he said.

"Are they all right?"

"George and Herb?"

"Who else?"

"Certainly, Irma; it's just the way they work."

"It's a comfort to know that," she said, "I'll shoo them in."

He settled back and watched the two come in. They sprawled themselves in chairs.

George shied a folder at him. "The Jenkins Dream; we got it all worked out."

"He's a jerk who wants to hunt big game," said Herb; we cooked up some dillies for him."

"We made it authentic," George declared with pride; we didn't skip a thing. We put him in the jungle, and we put in mud and insects and the heat; we crammed the place with ravenous nightmares. There's something thirsting for his blood behind every bush."

"It's no hunt," said Herb; "it's a running battle. When he isn't scared, he's jumpy. Damned if I can figure out a guy like that."

"It takes all kinds," said Blaine.

"Sure; and we get them all."

"Some day," Blaine told them drily, "you guys will lay it on so thick you'll get booted to Conditioning."

"They can't do that," said Herb. "You got to have a medical degree to get into Conditioning. And George and me, we couldn't bandage a finger the way it should be done."

George shrugged. "We haven't a thing to worry about; Myrt takes care of that. When we go too hog wild, she tames it down."

Blaine laid the folder to one side. "I'll feed it in before I leave tonight." He picked up the pad. "I have something different here. You'll have to slick down your hair and get on good behavior before I turn you loose on it."

"The one who just went out?"

Blaine nodded.

"I could cook up a Dream for her," said Herb.

"She wants peace and dignity," Blaine informed them. "Genteel society. A sort of modern version of mid-nineteenth century Old Plantation days. No rough stuff; just magnolia and white columns; horses in the bluegrass."

"Likker," said Herb. "Oceans of likker. Bourbon and mint leaves and . . ."

"Cocktails," Blaine told him, "and not too many of them."

"Fried chicken," said George, getting into the act. "Watermelon. Moonlight. River boats. Lemme at it."

"Not so fast; you have the wrong approach. Slow and easy. Tame down. Imagine slow music. A sort of eternal waltz."

"We could put in a war," said Herb; "they fought polite in those days. Sabers and all dressed up in fancy uniforms."

"She doesn't want a war."

"You gotta have *some* action."

"No action—or very little of it. No worry; no competition. Gentility . . ."

"And us," lamented George, "all spattered up with jungle mud."

The intercom buzzed. "The b.a. wants to see you," Irma said.

"O.K., tell him . . ."

"He wants to see you now."

"Oh, oh," said George.

"I always liked you, Norm," said Herb.

"All right," said Blaine. "Tell him I'll be right up."

"After all these years," Herb said, sadly. "Cutting throats and stabbing backs to get ahead and now it comes to this."

George drew his forefinger across his throat and made a hissing sound, like a blade slashing into flesh.

They were very funny.

2

Lew Giesey was the business agent of the Dream guild. For years he had run it with an iron fist and disarming smile. He was loyal and he demanded loyalty; he dealt out sharp, decisive discipline as quickly as he rewarded praise.

He worked in an ornate office, but behind a battered desk to which he clung stubbornly, despite all efforts to provide him with a better one. To him, the desk must have been a symbol—or a reminder—of the bitter struggle to attain his station. He had started with that desk in the early days; it had followed him from office to office as he fought his bare-knuckled way ahead, up the table of organization to the very top. The desk was scarred and battered, unlike the man himself. It was almost as if the desk, in the course of years, might have intervened itself to take the blows aimed at the man behind it.

But there had been one blow which it could not take for him. For Lou Giesey sat in his chair behind the desk and he was quite dead. His head had fallen forward on his chest and his forearms still rested on the chair's arms and his hands still clutched the wood.

The room was at utter peace and so, it seemed as well, the man behind the desk. There was a quietness in the room, as if respite had come from all the years of struggle and of planning. It rested now with a sense of urgency, as if it might have known that the respite could not last for long. In a little while, another man would come and sit behind the desk—perhaps a different one, for no other man would want Giesey's battered desk—and the struggle and the turmoil would start up again.

Norman Blaine stopped when he was halfway between the door and desk; it was the quietness of the room, as well as the head sunk upon the chest, that told him what had happened.

He stopped and listened to the soft whirring of the clock upon the wall, a sound usually lost until this moment in this place. He heard the almost-inaudible flutter of a typewriter from across the hall, the far-off, muffled rumble of wheels rushing along the highway that ran past the Center.

He thought, with one edge of his mind: *Death and peace and quiet, the three of them together, companions hand in hand.* Then his mind recoiled upon itself and built up into a tight coil spring of horror.

Blaine took a slow step forward, then another one, walking across the carpeting that allowed no footfall sound. He had not as yet realized the full impact of what had happened there—that moments before the business agent had asked to speak to him; that he was the one to find Giesey dead; that his presence in the office might lead to suspicion of him.

He reached the desk and the phone was there in front of him, on one corner of the desk. He lifted the receiver and when the switchboard voice came, he said: "Protection, please."

He heard the clicking as the signal was set up. "Protection."

"Farris, please."

Blaine started to shake, then—the muscles in his forearm jumping, others twitching in his face. He felt breathlessness rising in him, his chest constricting, a choking in his throat, and his mouth suddenly dry and sticky. He gritted his teeth and stopped the jumping muscles.

"Farris speaking."

"Blaine. Fabrication."

"Oh, yes, Blaine. What can I do for you?"

"Giesey called me up to see him; when I got here he was dead."

There was a pause—not too long a pause. Then: "You're sure he's dead."

"I haven't touched him. He's sitting in his chair; he looks dead to me."

"Anyone else know?"

"No one. Darrell is out in the reception room, but ..."

"You didn't yell out that he was dead."

"Not a word; I picked up the phone and called you."

"Good boy! That's using your head. Stay right there; don't tell anyone, don't let anyone in; don't touch anything. We're on our way."

The connection clicked and Norman Blaine put the receiver back into the cradle.

The room was still at rest, squeezing out of the next few moments all the rest it could. Soon the fury would take up again; Paul Farris and his goons would come bursting in.

Blaine stood by the corner of the desk, uncertainly—waiting, too. And now that he had the time to think, now that the shock had partially worn away and the acceptance

of the fact began to seep into his mind, new ideas came
creeping in to plague him.

He had found Giesey dead, but would they believe that
Blaine had found him dead? Would they ask Blaine how
he could prove that he had found Lew Giesey dead?

What did he want to see you for? they'd ask. How often
had Giesey called you in before? Do you have any idea
why he called you in this time?

Praise? Reprimand? Caution? Discussion of new techniques? Trouble in your department, maybe? Some devia-
tion in your work. How's your private life? Some
indiscretion that you had committed?

He sweated, thinking of the questions.

For Farris was thorough. You had to be thorough and
unrelenting—and tough—to head up Protection. You
were hated from the start, and fear was a necessary factor
to counteract the hatred.

Protection was necessary. The guild was an unwieldy
organization for all its tight efficiency, and it must be kept
in line. Intrigue must be rooted out. Deviationism—dicker-
ing with other unions—must be run down and have an end
put to it. There must be no wavering in the loyalty of any
members; and to effect all this, there was need of an iron
hand.

Blaine reached out to clutch at the desk, then remembered that Farris had told him not to touch a thing.

He pulled his hand back, let it hang by his side, and that
seemed awkward and unnatural. He put it in his pocket,
and that seemed awkward, too. He put both his hands
behind his back and clasped them, then teetered back and
forth.

He fidgeted.

He swung around to look at Giesey, wondering if the
head still rested on the chest, if the hands still gripped
the chair arms. For a moment, Norman Blaine built up
in his mind the little speculative fiction that Lew Giesey
would not be dead at all, but would have raised his head
and be looking at him. And if that were so, Blaine wondered how he would explain.

He needn't have wondered; Giesey still was dead.

And now, for the first time, Norman Blaine began to

see the man in relation to the room—not as a single point of interest, but as a man who sat in a chair, with the chair resting on the carpeting and the carpeting covering the floor.

Giesey's uncapped pen lay upon the desk in front of him, resting where it had stopped after rolling off a sheaf of papers. Giesey's spectacles lay beside the pen; off to one side was a glass with a little water left in the bottom of it; beside it stood the stopper of the carafe from which Giesey must recently have poured himself a drink.

And on the floor, beside Lew Giesey's feet, was a single sheet of paper.

Blaine stood there, staring at the paper, wondering what it was. It was a form of some sort, he could see, and there was writing on it. He edged around the desk to get a better look at it, egged on by an illogical curiosity.

He bent low to read the writing, and a name came up and struck him in the face. *Norman Blaine!*

He bent swiftly and scooped the paper off the carpet. It was an appointment form, dated the day before yesterday and it appointed Norman Blaine as Administrator of Records, Dream Department, effective as of midnight of this day. It was duly signed and stamped as having been recorded.

John Roemer's job, Blaine thought, the job that they had whispered about for weeks throughout the Center.

He had a fleeting moment of triumph. They'd picked him. He had been the man for the job! But there was more than triumph. He not only had the job, but he had the answers to the questions they would ask.

Why were you called in? they'd ask. Now he could answer them. With this paper in his pocket, he would have the answer.

But he didn't have much time.

He laid the paper on the desk and folded it one third over, forcing himself to take the time to do it neatly. Then, just as neatly, he folded the other one third over and thrust it in his pocket. Then he turned again to face the door and waited.

The next moment, Paul Farris and a half dozen of his goons came stamping in.

3

Farris was a smooth operator. He was a top-notch policeman and had the advantage of looking like a college instructor. He was not a big man; he wore his hair slicked down, and his eyes were weak and wavery back of the spectacles.

He settled himself comfortably in the chair behind his desk and laced his hands over his belly. "I'll have to ask you some questions," he told Blaine. "Just for the record, naturally. The death is an open-and-shut one of suicide. Poison. We won't know what kind until Doc gets the test run through."

"I understand," said Blaine.

And thought: *I understand, all right. I know just how you work. Lull a man to sleep, then belt him in the guts.*

"You and I have worked together for a long time," said Farris. "Not together, exactly, but under the same roof and for the same purpose. We've got along fine; I know that we will continue in exactly the same way."

"Why, certainly," said Blaine.

"This appointment form," said Farris; "you say you got it in an inter-office envelope."

Blaine nodded. "It was in my basket this morning, I suppose. I didn't get around to going through the stuff until rather late."

Which was true enough, he hadn't gone through the basket until 10 o'clock or so. And another thing—there was no record of inter-office mail.

And still another thing: Maintenance came around and emptied the waste baskets at precisely 11:30; it was now a quarter of one, and anything that had been in his basket had long since been burned.

"And you just put the form in your pocket and forgot about it?"

"I didn't forget about it; I had an applicant about that time. Then, when the applicant left, two of the fabricators came in. I was going over a point or two with them when Giesey called and asked me to come up."

22

Farris nodded. "You think he wanted to talk with you about your new position?"

"That was what I thought."

"Had he talked about it before? Did you know that it was coming?"

Norman Blaine shook his head. "It was a complete surprise."

"A happy one, of course?"

"Naturally. It's a better job. Better pay. A man wants to get ahead."

Farris looked thoughtful.

"Didn't it strike you as a rather strange procedure to get an appointment—particularly to a key position—in an inter-office envelope?"

"Of course it did; I wondered about it at the time."

"But you did nothing about it?"

"I have told you," Blaine said, "I was busy. And what would you suggest that I should have done?"

"Nothing," Farris told him.

"That is what I thought," said Blaine. He thought: *Make something out of it, if you can.*

He felt a brief elation and fought it down. It was too soon, he knew.

At the moment there wasn't a thing that Farris could do—not a single thing. The appointment was in order, properly signed and executed. As of the coming midnight he, Norman Blaine, would be administrator of records, taking over from Roemer. Only the delivery of the appointment was not in order, but there was no way in the world that Farris could prove that Blaine had not received it in the inter-office mail.

He wondered, briefly, what might have happened if Giesey had not died. Would the appointment have come through, or would it have been quashed somewhere along the line? Would some pressure have been brought to bear to give the position to someone else?

Farris was saying, "I knew the change was going to be made. Roemer was getting—well, just a little difficult. It had come to my attention, and I spoke to Giesey about it. So had several others. We talked about it some; he mentioned you as among several men who could be trusted, but that was all he said."

"You didn't know he had decided?"

Farris shook his head. "No, but I'm glad he picked you for the post. You're the kind of man I like to work with, realistic. We'll get along. We'd better talk about it."

"Any time," said Blaine.

"If you have the time, how about dropping in on me tonight? Any time at all, I'll be home all evening. You know where I live?"

Blaine nodded and got to his feet.

"Don't worry about this business," Farris said. "Lew Giesey was a good man, but there are other good men. We all thought a lot of him. I know it must have been a shock, walking in on him that way."

He hesitated for a moment, then: "And don't worry about any change in your appointment. I'll speak to whomever replaces Giesey."

"Any idea who it'll be?"

Farris' eyelids flicked just once, then his eyes were hard and steady, wavery no longer. "No idea," he said, brusquely. "The executive board will name the man. I have no idea who they'll put the finger on."

The hell you don't, thought Blaine.

"You're sure about it being suicide?"

"Certain," Farris said. "Giesey had a heart history, he was worried."

He rose and reached for his cap, put it on. "I like a man who thinks fast on his feet. Keep thinking on your feet, Blaine. We'll get along."

"I'm sure we will."

"Don't forget about tonight."

"I'll be seeing you," Blaine told him.

4

The Buttonholer had seized upon Norman Blaine that morning, after he had parked his car, just when he was leaving the lot. How the man had gotten in, Blaine could not imagine, but there he was, waiting for a victim. "Just a second, sir," he said.

Blaine swung around toward him. The man took a

quick step forward, put out both his hands and clasped Blaine's lapels firmly. Blaine backed away, but the man's fingers held their grip and halted him.

"Let me go," Blaine said, but the man told him, "Not until I've had a word with you. You work at the Center and you're just the man I want to talk with. Because if I can make you understand—why, then, sir, I know that there is hope.

"Hope," he said, a fine spray of saliva flying from between his lips—"hope that we can make the people understand the viciousness of Dreams. Because they are vicious, sir, they undermine the moral fiber of the people. They hold the opportunity for quick escape from the troubles and the problems which develop character. With the Dreams, there is no need for a man to face his troubles— he can run away from them, he can seek a forgetfulness in Dreams. I tell you, sir, it is the damnation of our culture."

Remembering it now, Norman Blaine still felt the cold, quiet whiteness of the anger that had enveloped him.

"Let loose of me," he'd said. There must have been something in his tone which warned the Buttonholer, for the man let loose his grip and backed away. And Blaine, lifting his arm to wipe his face upon his coat sleeve, watched him back away then finally turn and run.

It had been the first time he'd ever been seized upon by a Buttonholer, although he had heard of them often and had laughed them off.

Now, thinking back upon it, he was surprised at the impact of his encounter with a Buttonholer—his horror that here, finally, he had physical evidence that there were persons in the world who doubted the sincerity and the purpose of the Dreams.

He jerked himself away from his reverie; there were other more important things with which to concern himself. Giesey's death and the sheet of paper he had found upon the floor—the strange conduct of Farris. *Almost,* he thought, *as if there were a conspiracy between the two of us—as if he and I had been involved in some gigantic plot, now coming to fruition.*

He sat quietly behind his desk and tried to think it out.

Given a moment to consider, he was certain that he

would not have snatched the paper off the floor; given another moment for consideration, even after having seen what it was, he was certain that he would have dropped it back on the floor again. But there had been no time at all. Farris and his goons were already on their way and Blaine had stood defenseless in the office with a dead man, without an adequate explanation of why he should be there, without an adequate answer to any of the questions that they were sure to ask him.

The paper had given him a reason for being in the office, had given him the answer to the questions, had forestalled many other questions that would have been asked if he had not had the answer to the first ones.

Farris had said suicide.

Would it have been suicide or murder, Blaine wondered, if he had not had the paper in his pocket? If he had remained defenseless, would his luckless position have been used to explain Giesey's death?

Farris had said he liked a man who could think standing on his feet. And there was no doubt he did. For Farris himself was a man who could think standing on his feet, who could improvise and trim his course with each passing situation.

And he was not a man to trust.

Blaine wondered if the appointment still would have come through if he'd not been there to pick it off the carpet. Certainly he was not the sort of man Paul Farris would have picked to take over Roemer's job. Would Farris, finding the appointment on the floor, have destroyed it and forged another, appointing someone more to his liking to the post?

And, another question: What was the importance of the job? Why did it matter, or seem to matter so much, who was appointed to it? No one had said, of course, that it was important; but Farris had been interested and Paul Farris never was interested in unimportant things.

Could the appointment, in some way, have been linked with Lew Giesey's death? Blaine shook his head. There was no way that one could answer.

The important thing was that he had the appointment—that Giesey's death had not prevented its delivery, that for the moment at least Farris was willing to let the situation ride.

But, Norman Blaine warned himself, he could not afford to take Farris at face value. As steward of the guild, Paul Farris was a police official with a loyal corps of men, with wide discretion in carrying out his functions, politically-minded and unscrupulous, busily carving out a niche large enough to fit full-scale ambition.

More than likely Giesey's death fitted in with this ambition. It was not beyond reason that Farris might, in some small and hidden way, have contributed—if, in fact, he had not engineered it.

Suicide, he had said. Poison. Worried. Heart history. Easy words to say. Watch your step, Blaine told himself. Take it easy. Make no sudden moves. And be ready to duck. Especially—be ready to duck.

He sat quietly, letting the turmoil of speculation run out of his mind. *No use thinking of it,* he told himself. *No use at all right now*. Later, when and if he had some facts to go on—then would be the time to think.

He glanced at the clock and it was three fifteen. Too early to go home.

And there was work to do. Tomorrow he'd be moving up to another office, but today there still was work to do.

He picked up the Jenkins folder and looked at it. A big game hunt, the two zany fabricators had said. We gave him the works, they'd said, or words to that effect.

He flipped the folder open and ran through the first few pages, shuddering just a little.

No accounting for tastes, he thought.

He remembered Jenkins—a great, massive brute of a man who had bellowed out a flow of language that had made the office quake.

Well, maybe he can take it, Blaine thought. *Anyhow, it is what he asked for*.

He tucked the folder under his arm and went out into the reception room.

Irma said, "We just heard the word."

"About Giesey, you mean."

"No, we heard that earlier. We all felt badly; I guess everybody liked him. But I mean the word about you. It's all over now. Why didn't you tell us right away? We think it's wonderful."

"Why, thank you, Irma."

"We'll miss you, though."

"That is good of you."

"Why did you keep it secret? Why didn't you let us know?"

"I didn't know myself until this morning; I guess I got too busy. Then Giesey called."

"There were goons all over the place, going through the waste baskets. I think they even went through your desk. What was the matter with them?"

"Just curious." Blaine went out into the hall and the chill of fear crept up his spine with every step he took.

He had known it before, of course, with Farris' crack about thinking on one's feet, but this put the clincher on it. This left no doubt at all that Farris knew he'd lied.

Maybe there was some merit in it, after all, though. His lie and bluff put him, momentarily, into Farris' class—made Blaine the kind of man the goon leader was able to understand, the kind of man he could do business with.

But could he keep up the bluff? Could he be tough enough?

Keep cool, Blaine, he told himself. *No sudden moves. Ready to duck, although you can't let them know you are. Poker face,* he told himself—*the kind of face you use when you face an applicant.*

He tramped on and the coldness wore away.

Going down the stairs into Myrt's room, the old magic gripped him once again.

There she sat—the great machine of dreams, the ultimate in the fabrication of the imaginative details of man's wildest fantasies.

He stood in the silence of the place and felt the majesty and peace, the almost-tenderness, that he always felt— as if Myrt were some sort of protective mother-goddess to which one might flee for understanding and unquestioning refuge.

He tucked the folder more tightly under his arm and walked softly across the floor, fearing to break the hush of the place with an awkward, or a heavy footfall.

He mounted the stairs that led to the great keyboard,

and sat down in the traveling seat which would move at
the slightest touch to any part of the coding panels. He
clamped the open folder on a clipboard in front of him and
reached out to the query lever. He pressed it, and an indi-
cator winked a flashing green. The machine was clear, he
could feed in his data.

He punched in the identification and then he sat in
silence—as he often sat in silence there.

This he would miss, Blaine knew, when he moved up to
that other job. Here he was like a priest, a sort of com-
municant with a force that he reverenced, but could not
understand—not in its entirety. For no man could know
the structure of the dream machine in its entirety. It was
too vast and complicated a mechanism to be fixed in any
mind.

It was a computer with magic built into it, and freed
from the utter, straight-line logic of other, less fabulous
computers. It dealt in fantasy rather than in fact—it was
a gigantic plot machine that wove out of punched-in symbols and equations the strange stories of many different
lives. It took in code and equations and it dished out
dreams!

Blaine started to punch in the data from the folder
sheets, moving swiftly about the face of the coding panel
in the traveling chair. The panel began to twinkle with
many little lights and from the dream machine came the
first faint sounds of tripping relays, the hum of power
stirring through the mechanisms, the click of control
counters, the faint, far-off chattering of memory files being
probed, and the purr of narrative sequence channels
getting down to work.

He worked on in a tense, closed-in world of concentra-
tion, setting up the co-ordinates from sheet after sheet.
Time came to an end and there was no other world than
the panel with its myriad keys, and trips and buttons,
and its many flashing lights.

Finally he was done, the last sheet fluttered down to the
floor from the empty clipboard. Time took up again and
the room came into being. Norman Blaine sat limply,
shirt soaked with perspiration, hair damp against his fore-
head, hands resting in his lap.

The machine was thundering now. Lights flashed by the

thousands, some of them winking steadily, others running bright little sequences like lazy lightning flashes. The sound of power surged within the room, filling it to bursting, and yet beneath the hum of power could be heard the busy thumps and clicks and the erratic insane chattering of racing mechanisms.

Wearily Blaine got out of the chair and picked up the fallen sheets, bundling them together, helter-skelter, without regard to numbering, back into the folder.

He walked to the far end of the machine and stood staring for a moment at the glass-protected cabinet where tape was spinning on a reel. He watched the spinning tape, fascinated, as always, by the thought that upon the tape was impressed the seeming life of a dream that might last a century or a thousand years—a dream built with such sheer story-telling skill that it would never pall, but would be fresh and real until the very last.

He turned away and walked to the stairway, went halfway up, then turned and looked back.

It was his last dream, he knew, the last he'd ever punch; tomorrow he'd be on another job. He raised his arm in half salute.

"So long, Myrt," he said.

Myrt thundered back at him.

5

Irma had left for the day and the office was empty, but there was a letter, addressed to Blaine, propped against the ash tray on his desk. The envelope was bulky and distorted when he picked it up, it jangled.

Norman Blaine ripped it open and a ring, crowded full of keys, fell out of it and clattered on the desk. A sheet of paper slipped halfway out and stuck.

He pushed the keys to one side, took out the sheet of paper and unfolded it. There was no salutation. The note began abruptly: *I called to turn over the keys, but you were out and your secretary didn't know when you would be back. There seemed no point in staying. If*

*you should want to see me later, I am at your service.
Roemer.*

He let the note fall out of his hand and flutter to the
desk. He picked up the keys and tossed them up and
down, listening to them jangle, catching them in his
palm.

What would happen to John Roemer now, he wondered. Had a place been made for him, or hadn't Giesey
gotten around to appointing him to some other post?
Or had Giesey intended that man be out entirely? That
seemed unlikely, for the guild took care of its own; it
did not, except under extreme provocation, throw a man
out on his own.

And, for that matter, who would take over the direction of Fabrication? Had Lew Giesey died before he
could make an appointment? George or Herb—either
one of them—would be in line, but they hadn't said a
word. They would have said something, Blaine was
sure, if they had been notified.

He picked up the sheet of paper and read the note
again. It was noncommittal, completely deadpan; there
was nothing to be learned from it.

He wondered how Roemer might feel about being
summarily replaced, but there was no way of knowing;
the note certainly gave no clue. And *why* had he been
replaced? There had been rumors, all sorts of rumors,
about a shakeup in the Center, but the rumors had
stopped short of the reasons for the shakeup.

It seemed a little strange—this leaving of the keys,
the transfer of authority symbolized by the leaving of
the keys. It was as if Roemer had thrown them on
Blaine's desk, said: "There they are, boy; they're all
yours," and then had left without another word.

Just a little burned up, perhaps. Just a little hurt.

But the man had come in person. Why? Under ordinary circumstances, Blaine knew, Roemer would have
stayed to break in the man who was to succeed him,
then would have gone up to Records. But Roemer would
have stayed on until his successor knew the ropes.

These were not ordinary circumstances. Come to think
of it, they seemed to be turning out to be most extra-
ordinary.

It was a fouled-up mess, Norman Blaine told himself. Going through regular channels, it would have been all right—a normal operation, the shifts made without disruption. But the appointment had not gone through channels; and had Blaine not been the one to find Lew Giesey dead, had he not seen the paper on the floor, the appointment might not have gone through at all.

But the job was his—he'd stuck out his neck to get it and it was his. It was not something he had sought, but now that he had it, he'd keep it. It was a step up the ladder; it was advancement. It paid better, had more prestige, and put him closer to the top—third from the top, in fact, for the chain of command ran: business agent, Protection, and then Records.

He'd tell Harriet tonight—but, no, he kept forgetting; he'd not see Harriet tonight.

He put the keys in his pocket and picked up the note again. *If you should want to see me later, I am at your service.*

Protocol? he wondered. Or was there something that he might need to know? Something that needed telling?

Could it be that Roemer had come to tell him something and then had lost his nerve?

Blaine crumpled the note and hurled it to the floor. He wanted to get out, get away from Center, get out where he could try to think it out, plan what he was to do. He should clean out his desk, he knew, but it was late—far past quitting time. And there was his date with Harriet—no, damn it, he kept forgetting. Harriet had called and said she couldn't make it.

There'd be time tomorrow to clean out his desk. He took his hat and coat and went out to the parking lot.

An armed guard had replaced the regular attendant at the entrance to the lot. Blaine showed his identification.

"All right, sir," said the guard. "Keep an eye peeled, though. A suspendee got away."

"Got away?"

"Sure; just woke a week or two ago."

"He can't get far," said Blaine. "Things change; he'll give himself away. How long was he in Sleep?"

"Five hundred years, I think."

"Things change a lot in five hundred years. He hasn't got a chance."

The guard shook his head. "I feel sorry for him. Must be tough, waking up like that."

"It's tough, all right. We try to tell them, but they never listen."

"Say," said the guard, "you're the one who found Giesey."

Blaine nodded.

"Was it the way they tell it? Was he dead when you got there?"

"He was dead."

"Murdered?"

"I don't know."

"It does beat hell. You get up to the top, then poof . . ."

"It does beat hell," agreed Blaine.

"You never know."

"No, you never do." Blaine hurried off.

He drove out of the lot and swung onto the highway. Dusk was just beginning and the road was almost deserted.

Norman Blaine drove slowly, watching the autumn countryside slide past. The first lamps glimmered from the windows of the villas set upon the hills; there was the smell of burning leaves and of the slow, sad dying of the year.

Thoughts flitted at him, like the skimming birds hurrying to a night-time tree, but he batted them away—the Buttonholer who had grabbed him—what Farris might suspect or know and what he might intend to do—why John Roemer had called personally to deliver the keys, and then had decided not to wait—why a suspendee should escape.

And that last one was a funny deal; it was downright crazy, when you thought about it. What could possibly be gained by such an escape, such a fleeing out into an alien world for which one was not prepared? It would be like going to an alien planet all alone without adequate briefing. It would be like walking onto a job with which one had no acquaintance and trying to bluff one's way.

I wonder why, he thought. *I wonder why he did it.*

He brushed the thought away; there was too much to think of. He'd have to get it straightened out before he could think it through. He could not allow himself to get the thoughts all cluttered up.

He reached out to the dash and turned on the radio.

A commentator was saying: "... who know their political history can recognize the crisis points that now are becoming more clearly defined. For more than five hundred years, the government, in actuality, has been in the hands of the Central Labor Union. Which is to say that the government is ruled by committee, with each of the guilds and unions represented on the central group. That such a group should be able to continue in control for five full centuries—for the last 60 years in openly admitted control—is not so much to be attributed to wisdom, forebearance or patience, as to a fine balance of power which has obtained within the body at all times. Mutual distrust and fear have at no time allowed any one union or guild or any combination to become dominant. As soon as one group threatened to become so, the personal ambitions of other groups operated to undermine the ascendant group.

"But this, as everyone must recognize, is a situation which has lasted longer than could normally have been expected. For years the stronger unions have been building up their strength—and not trying to use it. You may be sure that none of them will attempt to use their strength until they're absolutely sure of themselves. Just where any of them stand, strength-wise, is impossible to say, for it is not good strategy that any union should let its strength be known. The day cannot be too far distant when there must be a matching of this strength. The situation, as it stands, must seem intolerable to some of the stronger unions with ambitious leaders ..."

Blaine turned off the radio and was astonished at the solemn peace of the autumn evening. It was all old stuff, anyway. So long as he could remember, there had been commentators talking thus. There were eternal rumors which at one time would name Transportation as the union that would take over, and at another time would hint at Communications, and at still another time would insist—just as authoritatively—that Food was the one to watch.

Dreams, he told himself smugly, were beyond that kind of politics. The guild—his guild—stood for public service. It was represented on Central, as was its right and duty, but it had never played at politics.

It was Communications that was always stirring up a fuss with articles in the papers and blatting commentators. If he didn't miss his guess, Blaine told himself, Communications was the worst of all—in there every minute waiting for its chance. Education, too; Education was always fouling up the detail, and what a bunch of creeps!

He shook his head, thinking of how lucky he was to be with Dreams—not to have to feel a sense of guilt when the rumors came around. You could be sure that Dreams never would be mentioned; of all the unions, Dreams was the only one that could stand up straight and tall.

He'd argued with Harriet about Communications, and at times she had gotten angry with him; she seemed to have the stubborn notion that Communications was the union which had the best public service record and the cleanest slate.

It was natural, of course, Blaine admitted, that one should think his own particular union was all right. Unions were the only loyalty to which a man could cling. Once, long ago, there had been nations and the love of one's own nation was known as patriotism. But now the unions had taken their place.

He drove into the valley that wound among the hills, and finally turned off the highway and followed the winding road that climbed into the hills.

Dinner would be waiting and Ansel would be cross (he was a cranky robot at the best). Philo would be waiting for him at the gate and they'd ride in together.

He passed Harriet's house and stared briefly at it, set well back among the trees, but there were no lights. Harriet wasn't home. An assignment, she had said; an interview with someone.

He turned in at his own gate and Philo was there, barking out his heart. Norman Blaine slowed the car and the dog jumped in, reached up to nuzzle his master's cheek just once, then settled sedately in the seat while they wheeled around the drive to stop before the house.

Philo leaped out quickly and Blaine got out more slowly. It had been a tiring day, he told himself. Now that he was home, he suddenly was tired.

He stood for a moment, looking at the house. It was a good house, he thought; a good place for a family—if he ever could persuade Harriet to give up her news career.

A voice said: "All right. You can turn around now. And take it easy; don't try any funny stuff."

Slowly Blaine turned. A man stood beside the car in the gathering dusk. He held a glinting object in his hand and he said, "There's nothing to be afraid of; I don't intend you any harm. Just don't get gay about it."

The man's clothes were wrong; they seemed to be some sort of uniform. And his words were wrong. The inflection was a bit off color, concise and crisp, lacking the slurring of one word into another which marked the language. And the phrases—*funny stuff; don't get gay*.

"This is a gun I have. No monkey business, please."

Monkey business.

"You are the man who escaped," said Blaine.

"That I am."

"But how . . ."

"I rode all the way with you. Hung underneath the car; those dumb cops didn't think to look."

The man shrugged. "I regretted it once or twice. You drove further than I hoped. I almost let go a time or two."

"But me? Why did you . . ."

"Not you, mister; anyone at all. It was a way to hide— a means to get away."

"I don't read you," Blaine told him. "You could have made a clean break; you could have let go at the gate. The car was going slow then. You could have sneaked away right now. I'd never noticed you."

"And been picked up as soon as I showed myself. The clothes are a giveaway. So is my speech. Then there's my eating habits, and maybe even the way I walk. I would stick out like a bandaged thumb."

"I see," said Blaine. "All right, then; put up the gun. You must be hungry. We'll go in and eat."

The man put away the gun. He patted his pocket. "I still have it, and I can get it fast. Don't try any swifties."

"O.K.," said Blaine. "No swifties." Thinking: Picturesque. *Swifties.* Never heard the word. But it had a meaning; there could be no doubt of that.

"By the way, how did you get that gun?"

"That's something," said the man, "I'm not telling you."

6

His name, the fugitive said, was Spencer Collins. He'd been in suspension for five hundred years; he'd come out of it just a month before. Physically, he said, he was as good a man as ever—fifty-five, and well preserved. He'd paid attention to himself all his life—had eaten right, hadn't gone without sleep, had exercised both mind and body, knew something about psychosomatics.

"I'll say this for your outfit," he told Blaine, "you know how to take care of a sleeper's body. I was a little gaunt when I came out; a little weak; but there'd been no deterioration."

Norman Blaine chuckled. "We're at work at it constantly. I don't know anything about it, of course, but the biology boys are at it all the time—it's a continuing problem with them. A practical problem. During your five hundred years you probably were shifted a dozen times or more—to a better receptacle each time, with improvements in the operation. You got the benefit of the new improvements as soon as we worked them out."

Collins had been a professor of sociology, he said, and he'd evolved a theory. "You'll excuse me if I don't go into what it was."

"Why certainly," said Blaine.

"It's not of too much interest except to the academic mind. I presume you're not an academic mind."

"I suppose I'm not."

"It involved long-term social development," Collins told him. "I figured that five hundred years should show some indication of whether I had been right or wrong. I was curious. It's rough to figure out a thing, then up and die without ever knowing if it comes true or not."

"I can understand."

"If you doubt me in any detail you can check the record."

"I don't doubt a word of it," said Blaine.

"You are used to screwball cases."

"Screwball?"

"Loopy. Crazy."

"I see many screwball cases," Blaine assured him.

But nothing quite so screwball as this, he thought. Nothing quite so crazy as sitting on the patio beneath the autumn stars, on his own home acres, talking to a man five centuries out of time. If he were in Readjustment, of course, he'd be accustomed to it, would not think it strange at all; Readjustment worked continually with cases just like this.

Collins was fascinating. His inflection betrayed the change in the spoken language, and there were those slang words always cropping up—idioms of the past that had somehow missed fire and found no place within the living language, although many others had survived.

At dinner there had been dishes the man had tackled with distrust, others that he'd eaten with disgust showing on his face, yet too polite to refuse them outright—determined, perhaps, to do his best to fit into the culture in which he found himself.

There were certain little mannerisms and affections that seemed pointless now; performed too often, they could become distinctly irritating. These were actions like stroking his chin when he was thinking, or popping joints by pulling at his fingers. That last one, Blaine told himself, was unnerving and indecent. Perhaps in the past it had not been ill-bred to fiddle with one's body. He'd have to look that one up, he told himself, or maybe ask someone. The boys in Readjustment would know—they'd know a lot of things.

"I wonder if you'd tell me," Blaine asked,—"this theory of yours. Did it work out the way you thought it would?"

"I don't know. You'll agree, perhaps, that I've scarcely been in a position to find out."

"I suppose that's true. But I thought you might have asked."

"I didn't ask," said Collins.

They sat in the evening silence, looking out across the valley.

"You've come a long way in the last five hundred years," Collins finally said. "When I went to sleep, we were speculating on the stars and everyone was saying that the light speed limit had us licked on that. But today . . ."

"I know," said Blaine. "Another five hundred years . . ."

"You could go on forever and forever—'sleep a thousand years and see what had happened. Then another . . ."

"It wouldn't be worth it."

"You're telling me," said Collins.

A nighthawk skimmed above the trees and planed into the sky in jerky, fluttering motions, busy catching insects. "That doesn't change," said Collins. "I can remember nighthawks . . ."

He paused, then asked, "What are you going to do with me?"

"You're my guest."

"Until the keepers come."

"We'll talk about it later; you are safe tonight."

"There is one thing you've been wondering about; I've watched it gnawing at you."

"Why you ran away."

"That is it," said Collins.

"Well?"

"I chose a dream," said Collins, "such as you might expect. I asked a professorial retreat—a sort of idealized monastery where I could spend my time in study, where I could live with other men who could talk my language. I wanted peace—a walk along a quiet river, a good sunset, simple food, time for reading and for thinking . . ."

Blaine nodded appreciatively. "A good choice, Collins; there should be more like it."

"I thought so, too," said Collins. "It was what I wanted."

"It proved enjoyable?"

"I wouldn't know."

"Wouldn't know?"

"I never got it."

"But the Dream was fabricated . . ."

"I got a different dream."

"There was some mistake."

"No mistake," said Collins; "I am sure there wasn't."

"When you ask a certain dream," Blaine began, speaking stiffly, but Collins cut him short. "There was no mistake, I tell you. The dream was substituted."

"How could you know that?"

"Because the dream they gave me wasn't one that anyone would ask for. Not even one that ever would be thought of. It was one that was deliberately tailored for some reason I can't figure out. It was a different world."

"An alien world!"

"Not alien; it was Earth, all right—but a different culture. I lived five hundred years in that world, every minute of five hundred years. The dream pattern was not shortened as I understand they often are, telescoping a thousand years of Sleep into a normal lifetime. I got the works, the full five hundred years. I know what the score is when I tell you that it was a deliberately fashioned dream—no mistake at all—but fashioned for a purpose."

"Now let's not rush ahead so fast," protested Blaine. "Let us take it easy. The world had a different culture?"

"It was a world," said Collins, "in which the profit motive had been eliminated, in which the concept of profit never had been thought of. It was the same world that we have, but lacking in all the factors and forces which in our world stem from the profit motive. To me, of course, it was utterly fantastic, but to the natives of the place—if you can call them that—it seemed the normal thing."

He watched Blaine closely. "I think you'll agree," he said, "that no one would want to live in a world like that. No one would ask a Dream like that."

"Some economist, perhaps . . ."

"An economist would know better. And, aside from

that, there was a terribly consistent pattern to the dream that no one without prior knowledge could ever figure out to put into a dream."

"Our machine . . ."

"Your machine would have no more prior knowledge than you yourself. No more, at least, than your best economist. And another thing—that machine is illogical; that's the beauty of it. It needn't think in logic. It shouldn't, because that would spoil the Dream. A Dream should not be logical."

"And yours was logical?"

"Very logical," said Collins. "You can figure out the factors hell to breakfast and you can't tell what will happen until you see a thing in action. That is logic for you."

He rose and walked across the patio, then walked back again, stood facing Blaine. "That's why I ran away. There's something dirty going on; I can't trust that gang of yours."

"I don't know," said Blaine. "I simply do not know."

"I can clear out if you want me to; no need to get yourself messed up in a deal like this. You took me in and fed me, gave me clothes, and you listened to me. I don't know how far I can get, but . . ."

"No," said Blaine, "you're staying here. This is something that needs investigation, and I may need you later on. Keep out of sight. Don't mind the robots. We can trust them; they won't talk."

"If they smell me out," said Collins, "I'll manage to get off your land before they nab me. Caught, I'll keep my mouth shut."

Norman Blaine rose slowly and held out his hand. Collins took it in a swift, sure grip. "It's a deal."

"It's a deal," echoed Blaine.

7

At night, the Center was a place of ghosts, its deserted corridors ringing with their emptiness. Men worked throughout the building, Blaine knew—the Readjustment force; the Conditioners; the Tank Room gang, but there was no sign of them.

A robot guard stepped out of his embrasure. "Who goes there?"

"Blaine. Norman Blaine."

The robot stood for a second, whirring gently, searching through its memory banks to find the name of Blaine. "Identification," it said.

Blaine held up his identification disk. "Pass, Blaine," the robot said, then tried an amenity. "Working late?"

"Something I forgot," Blaine told it.

He went along the corridor and took the elevator, got out at the sixth.

Another robot stopped him. He identified himself.

"You're on the wrong floor, Blaine."

"New appointment." He showed the robot the form.

"All right, Blaine," it said.

Blaine went along the corridor and found the door to Records. He tried six keys before he hit the right one and the door swung open.

He closed the door behind him and waited until he could see a little before he found the light switch.

There was a front office; off it, a door led into the record stacks. What he sought should be here somewhere, Blaine told himself. Myrt would have finished it hours before—the Jenkins dream of big game hunting in the steaming jungle.

It would not have been filed as yet, might not be filed at all, for Jenkins would be coming in to take the Sleep in just a day or two. Perhaps there was a rack somewhere where the dreams-to-be-called-for were placed against their use.

He walked around a desk and looked about the room. Filing cabinets, more desks, a testing cubicle, a drink and lunch dispenser, and a rack in which were stacked half a dozen reels.

He walked swiftly to the rack and picked up the first reel. He found the Jenkins Dream five reels down and stood with it in his hand, wondering just how insane a man could get.

Collins must be mistaken, or there had been some mistake—or it was all a lie, directed to what purpose he had no idea. It simply couldn't be, Blaine told himself, that a dream would be deliberately substituted.

But he had come this far. Thus far he had a made a fool out of himself . . .

He shrugged; he might just as well go all the way now that he was here.

Reel in hand, Norman Blaine walked into the testing cubicle and closed the door behind him. He inserted the reel and set the time at thirty minutes; then he put the cap upon his head and lay down upon the bed. Reaching out, he turned on the mechanism.

There was a faint whirring of the mechanism. Something puffed into his face and the whirr was gone; the cubicle was gone and Blaine stood in a desert, or what seemed to be a desert.

The landscape was red and yellow; there was a sun, and heat rose up from sand and rocks to strike him in the face. He raised his head to stare out at the horizons and saw that they lay far distant, for the land was flat. A lizard ran, squeaking, from the shade of one rock to the shadow of another. Far in the hot silk-blue of the sky a bird was circling.

He saw that he stood upon a road of sorts; it wound across the desert's face until it was lost in the heat-wavers that rose up from the tortured ground. And far off on the road a black speck travelled slowly.

He looked around for shade and there was no shade, nothing big enough to cast a shadow for anything bigger than the scuttling, squeaking lizard.

Blaine lifted his hands and looked at them; they were tanned so deeply, that for a moment, he thought that they were black. He wore a pair of ragged trousers, chewed off between knee and ankle and a tattered shirt, plastered to his back with sweat. He wore no shoes, and wondered about that until he lifted his feet and saw the horn-like callouses that had grown upon them to protect them from the heat and rocks.

Wondering dimly what he might be doing here, what he had been doing a moment before, what he was supposed to do, Norman Blaine stood and stared off across the desert. There was not a thing to see—just the red and yellow and the sand and heat.

He shuffled his feet in the sand, digging holes with his toes, then smoothing them out again with the flat of his calloused feet. Then the memory of who he was, and what he had meant to do, came seeping slowly back. It came in snatches and in driblets, and a great deal of it did not seem to make much sense.

He had left his home village that morning to travel to a city. There was some important reason why he should make the trip, although for the life of him he could not think of the reason. He had come from thataway and he was going thisaway; he wished that he could at least remember the name of his home village. It would be embarrassing if he met someone who asked him where he hailed from, and he could not tell them. He wished, too, that he could remember the name of the city he was going to, but that didn't matter quite so much. After a time, he'd get there and learn the name.

He started down the road, going thisaway, and he seemed to remember that he had a long way to travel yet. Somehow or other, he'd fooled around and lost a lot of time; it behooved him to get a hustle on if he expected to reach the city before nightfall.

He saw the black dot moving on the road and now it seemed much closer.

He was not afraid of the black dot and that was encouraging, he told himself. But when he tried to figure out why it should be so encouraging, Blaine simply couldn't say.

And because he had wasted a lot of time and had a long way yet to go, he broke into a trot. He legged it down the road as fast as he could go, despite the roughness of the trail and the hotness of the sun. As he ran he slapped his pockets and found that in one of them he carried certain objects. He knew immediately that the objects were of more than ordinary value; in a little while, he'd know what the objects were.

The black dot drew nearer; finally, it was close enough so that Blaine could see it was a large cart with wooden wheels. It was drawn by a fly-blown camel; a man sat upon the seat of the cart, beneath a tattered umbrella that, at one time, might have been colorful but now was bleached by the sun to a filthy gray.

He approached the cart, still running, and finally drew abreast of it. The man yelled something at the camel, which stopped.

"You took your time," he said. "Now get up here; get a wiggle on."

"I was detained," said Blaine.

"You were detained," sneered the other man, and thrust the reins at Blaine, jumping off the cart.

Blaine yelled at the camel and slapped him with the reins; he wondered what in hell was going on, and he was back in the cubicle again. His shirt was stuck against his back with perspiration, and he could feel the heat of the desert sun fading from his face.

He lay for a long moment, gathering his wits, reorienting himself. Beside him the reel moved slowly, bunching up the tape against the helmet slot. Blaine reached out a hand and stopped it, slowly spun it backwards to take up the tape.

There the horror of it dawned upon him, and for a moment he was afraid that he might cry out; but the cry died in his throat and he lay there motionless, frozen with the realization of what had happened.

He swung his feet off the cot and jerked the reel from its holder, stripping the tape out of the helmet. He turned the reel on its side and read the number and the name. The name was Jenkins, and the number was the identifying code he'd punched into the dream machine that very afternoon. There could be no mistake about it. The reel held the Jenkins dream. It was the reel that would be sent down in another day or two, when Jenkins came to take the Sleep.

And Jenkins, who had hankered for a big-game hunting trip, who had wanted to spend the next two hundred years on a shooting orgy, would find himself standing in a red and yellow desert on a track that could be called a road only by the utmost courtesy; in the distance he would see a moving dot, that would turn out later to be a camel and a cart.

He'd find himself in a desert with ragged pants and tattered shirt and with something in his pocket of more than ordinary value—but there would be no jungles and no veldt; there'd be no guns and no safari. There's be no hunting trip at all.

How many others? Blaine asked himself. *How many others failed to get the dream they wanted?* And what was more: *Why had they failed to get the dream they wanted?*

Why had the dreams been substituted?

Or *had* they been substituted? Had Myrt—

He shook his head at that one. The great machine did what it was told. It took in the symbols and equations and it chattered and it clanked and it thundered, and it spun the dream that was asked of it.

Substitution was the only answer, for the dreams were monitored in this very cubicle. No dream went out until someone had checked to see that it was the dream ordered by the Sleeper.

Collins had lived out five hundred years in a world which lacked the profit concept. And the red and yellow desert—what kind of world was that? Norman Blaine had not been there long enough to know; but there was one thing he did know—that, like Collins' world, the Jenkins world was one no one would ask to live in.

The cart had wooden wheels and had been pulled by camel-power; that might mean that it was a world in which the idea of mechanized transportation never had been thought of. But it might, as well, be any one of a thousand other kinds of cultures.

Blaine open the door of the cubicle and went out. He put the reel back in the rack and stood for a moment in the center of the icy room. After a moment, he realized that it was not the room that was icy, but himself.

This afternoon, when he had talked with Lucinda Silone Blaine had thought of himself as a dedicated person, had thought of the Center and the guild as a place of dedication. He had talked unctuously of the fact there must be no taint upon the guild, that it must at all times perform its services so as to merit the confidence of anyone who might apply for Sleep.

And where was that dedication now? Where was the public confidence?

How many others had been given substituted dreams?

How long had this been going on? Five hundred years ago, Spencer Collins had been given a dream that was not the dream he wanted. So the tampering had been going on five hundred years, at least.

And how many others in the years to come?

Lucinda Silone—what kind of dream would she get? Would it be the mid-nineteenth century plantation or some other place? How many of the dreams that Blaine had helped in fabricating had been changed?

He thought of the girl who had sat across the desk from him that morning—the honey color hair and the blue eyes, the milky whiteness of her skin, the way she talked, the things she had said, and the others that she had not said.

She, too, he thought.

And there was an answer to that. He moved swiftly toward the door.

8

He climbed the steps and rang the bell; a voice told him to come in.

Lucinda Silone sat in a chair beside a window. There was only one light—a dim light—in the far corner of the room, so that she sat in shadow. "Oh, it's you," she said. "You do the investigating, too."

"Miss Silone . . ."

"Come in and have a seat. I'm quite willing to answer any questions; you see, I am still convinced . . ."

"Miss Silone," said Blaine, "I came to tell you not to take the Sleep. I came to warn you; I have . . ."

"You fool," she said. "You utter, silly fool."

"But . . ."

"Get out of here," she told him.

"But it's . . ."

She rose out of her chair and there was scorn in every line of her. "So I can't take a chance. Go ahead; tell me it's dangerous. Go on and tell me it's a trick. You fool—I knew all that before I ever came."

"You know . . ."

They stood for a moment in tense silence, each staring at the other. "And now *you* know." And she said something else he had thought himself not half an hour before: "How about that dedication now?"

"Miss Silone, I came to tell you . . ."

"Don't tell anyone," she said. "Go back home and forget you know it; you'll be more comfortable that way. Not dedicated, maybe, but much more comfortable. And you'll live a good deal longer."

"There is no need to threaten . . ."

"Not a threat, Blaine; just a tip. If word should get to Farris that you know, you could count your life in hours. And I could see that the tip got round to Farris. I know just the way to do it."

"But Farris . . ."

"He's dedicated, too?"

"Well, no, perhaps not. I don't . . ."

The thought was laughable. Paul Farris dedicated!

"When I come back to Center," she said, speaking evenly and calmly, "we'll proceed just as if this had never happened. You'll make it your personal business to see that my Sleep goes through, without a hitch. Because if you don't, word will get to Farris."

"But why is it so important that you take the Sleep, knowing what you do?"

"Maybe I'm Entertainment," she said. "You rule out Entertainment, don't you? You asked me if I was Entertainment and you were very foxy while you were doing it. You fob off Entertainment because you're afraid they'll steal your Dreams for solidiographs. They tried to do it once, and you've been jumpy ever since."

"You're not Entertainment."

"You thought so this morning. Or was that all an act?"

"It was an act," Blaine admitted miserably.

"But this tonight isn't an act," she said coldly, "because you're scared as you've never been before. Well, keep on being scared. You have a right to be."

She stood for a moment, looking at him in disgust. "And now get out."

Philo did not meet him at the gate, but ran out of a clump of shrubbery, barking in high welcome, when he swung the car around the circle drive and stopped before the house. "Down, Philo," Blaine told him. "Down."

He climbed out of the car and Philo moved, quietly now, to stand beside him; in the quietness of the night, he could hear the click of the dog's toenails upon the bluestone walk. The house stood large and dark, although a light burned beside the door. He wondered how it was that houses and trees always seemed larger in the night, as if with the coming of the dark they took on new dimensions.

A stone crunched underneath a foot step and he swung around. Harriet stood on the path. "I was waiting for you," she said. "I thought you'd never come. Philo and I were waiting, and ..."

"You gave me a start," he told her. "I thought that you were working."

She moved swiftly forward and the light from the entrance lamp fell across her face. She was wearing a low-cut dress that sparkled in the light, and a sparkling veil was flung across her head so that it seemed she was surrounded by a thousand twinkling stars. "There was someone here," she told him.

"Someone ..."

"I drove up the back way. There was a car out front, and Philo was barking. I saw three of them come out the door, dragging a fourth. He was fighting and struggling, but they hurried him along and pushed him in the car. Philo was nipping at them, but they paid him no attention, they were in such a hurry. I thought at first it might be you, but then I saw it wasn't. The three were dressed like goons and I was a little frightened. I sped up and drove past and tore out on the highway, as fast as I could go, and ..."

"Now, wait a minute," Blaine cautioned. "You're going too fast; take your time and tell me ..."

"Then, later, I drove back, without my lights, and parked the car at my place. I came across the woods and I've been waiting for you."

She paused, breathless with her rush of words.

He reached out, put his fingers underneath her chin, tipped up her face and kissed her.

She brushed his hand away. "At a time like this," she said.

"Any time, at all."

"Norm, are you in trouble? Is someone after you?"

"There may be several who are after me."

"And you stand around and slobber over me."

"I just happened to think," he said, "of what I have to do."

"What do you have to do?"

"Go see Farris. He invited me; I forgot until just now."

"But you forget. I said goons . . ."

"They weren't goons. They were dressed to look like goons."

For now, suddenly, Norman Blaine saw it as a single unit with a single purpose—saw at last the network of intrigue and of purpose that he had sought since that morning.

First, there had been the Buttonholer who had collared him; then Lucinda Silone who had wished a dream of dignity and peace; and after that, Lew Giesey, dead behind his battered desk—and finally the man who had spent five hundred years in a culture that had not discovered a profit.

"But Farris . . ."

"Paul Farris is a friend of mine."

"He is no one's friend."

"Just like that," said Blaine, thrusting out two fingers, pressed very close together.

"I'd be careful just the same."

"Since this afternoon, Farris and I are conspiratorial pals. We are in a deal together; Giesey died . . ."

"I know. What has that to do with this sudden friendship?"

"Before he died, Giesey put an appointment through. I'm moving up to Records."

"Oh, Norm. I'm so glad!"

"I had hoped you'd be."

"Then what is it all about?" she asked. "Tell me what is going on. Who was that man the goons dragged out of here?"

"I told you—they weren't goons."

"Who was the man. Don't try to duck the question."

"An escapee. A man who ran away from Center."

"And you were helping him."

"Well, no . . ."

"Norm, why should anyone want to escape from Center? Have you got folks locked up?"

"This one was an awakened suspendee . . ."

He knew he'd said too much, but it was too late. He saw the glint in her eyes—the look he'd grown to know. "It's not a story," he said. "If you use this . . ."

"That's what you think."

"This was in confidence."

"Nothing's in confidence; you can't talk to News in confidence."

"You'd just be guessing."

"You'd better tell me now," she said. "I can find out, anyhow."

"That old gag!"

"You may as well go ahead and tell me. It'll save me a lot of trouble, and you'll know I have it straight."

"Not another word."

"All right, smart guy," she said.

She stood on tiptoe, kissed him swiftly, then ducked away.

"Harriet!" he cried, but she had stepped back into the shadow of the shrubbery and was gone. He took a quick step forward, then halted. There was no use going after her. He could never find or catch her, for she knew the gardens and the woods that stretched between their houses fully as well as he did.

Now he'd let himself in for it. By morning, the story would be in the papers.

He knew that Harriet had meant exactly what she said. Damn the woman. Fanatical, he told himself. Why couldn't she see things in their right perspective? Her loyalty to Communications was utterly fantastic.

And yet it was no more so than Norman Blaine's to Dreams. What had the commentator said when he'd been driving home? The unions were building up their strength, and it was this very fanatic loyalty—his to Dreams, Harriet's to Communications—which was the basis of that growing strength.

He stood in the puddle of light before the door and shivered at the thought of the story with 96-point headlines screaming from Page One.

Not a breath of scandal, he had said that afternoon. For Dreams was built on public confidence; any hint of scandal would bring it tumbling down. And here was scandal—or something that could be made to sound very much like scandal.

There were two things he could do. He could try to stop Harriet—how, he did not know. Or he could unmask this intrigue for what it really was—a plot to eliminate Dreams in the struggle for power, a move in that Central Labor struggle about which the commentator had held forth so pontifically.

Now Blaine was sure that he knew how it all tied up, was sure that he could trace the major plot-lines that ran through these fantastic happenings. But if he meant to prove what he suspected, he didn't have much time. Harriet was already off on a hunt for the facts of which he'd given her a hint. Perhaps she'd not have them for the morning editions, but by evening the story would be broken.

And before that happened, Dreams must have its story to combat the flying rumors.

There was one fact he had to verify. A man should know his history, Blaine told himself. It should not be a thing to be looked up in books, but carried in one's head, a ready tool for use.

Lucinda Silone had said she was Education and she would have told the truth. That was something which could be checked, one of the facts that would be checked automatically. Spencer Collins was Education, too. A professor of sociology, he had said, who had evolved a theory.

There was something in the history of the guilds concerning Dreams and Education, something about a connection that had once existed between them—and it might apply.

He went swiftly up the walk and through the hall, trudging down the hall to the study, with Philo following after. He thumbed up the switch and went quickly to the shelves. He ran a finger along a row of books until he found the one he wanted.

At the desk, he turned on the lamp and ran quickly through the pages. He found what he wanted—the fact he'd known was there, read long ago and forgotten, dimmed out by the years of never being needed.

10

Farris' house was surrounded by a great metallic wall, too high to jump, too smooth to climb. A guard was posted at the gate and another at the door.

The first guard frisked Blaine; the second demanded identification. When he was satisfied, he called a robot to take the visitor to Farris.

Paul Farris had been drinking. The bottle on the table beside his chair was better than half empty. "You took your time in coming," he growled.

"I got busy."

"Doing what, my friend?"

Farris pointed at the bottle. "Help yourself. There are glasses in the rack."

Blaine poured out liquor until the glass was almost full. He said casually, "Giesey was murdered, wasn't he?"

The liquor in Farris' glass slopped slightly, but there was no other sign. "The verdict was suicide."

"There was a glass on the desk," said Blaine. "He'd just had a drink out of the carafe; there was poison in the water."

"Why don't you tell me something I don't know?"

"And you're covering up for someone."

"Could be," Farris said. "Could be, too, it's none of your damn business."

"I was just thinking. Education . . ."

"What's that!"

"Education has been carrying a knife for us for a long time now. I looked up the history of it. Dreams started as a branch of Education, a technique for learning while you were asleep. But we got too big for them, and we got some new ideas—a thousand years ago. So we broke away, and . . ."

"Now, wait a minute; say that slow, again."

"I have a theory."

"You have a head, too, Blaine. A good imagination. That's what I said this afternoon; you think standing."

Farris lifted his glass and emptied it in a single gulp. "We'll stick the knife into them," he said, dispassionately. "Clear up to their gizzard."

Still dispassionately, he hurled the glass against the wall. It exploded into dust. "Why the hell couldn't someone have thought of that to start with? It would have made it simple . . . Sit down, Blaine. I think we got it made."

Blaine sat down and suddenly was sick—sick at the realization that he had been wrong. It was not Education which had engineered the murder. It had been Paul Farris—Farris and how many others? For no one man—even with the organization the goon leader had at his command—could have worked on a thing like this alone.

"One thing I want to know," said Farris. "How did you get that appointment? You didn't get it the way you said; you weren't meant to get it."

"I found it on the floor; it fell off Giesey's desk."

There was no need of lying any longer, of lying or pretending. There was no further need of anything; the old pride and loyalty were gone. Even as Norman Blaine thought about it, the bitterness sank deeper into his soul; the futility of all the years was a torture that rasped across raw flesh.

Farris chuckled. "You're all right," he said. "You could have kept your mouth shut and made it stick. It takes guts to do a thing like that. We can work together."

"It still is sticking," Blaine told him sharply. "Take it away from me if you think you can."

This was sheer bravado and bitterness, a feeble hitting

back, and Blaine wondered why he did it, for the job meant nothing now.

"Take it easy," Farris said. "You're keeping it. I'm glad it worked out as it did. I didn't think you had it in you, Blaine; I guess that I misjudged you."

He reached for the bottle. "Hand me another glass."

Blaine handed him another glass and Farris filled both. "How much do you know?"

Blaine shook his head. "Not too much. This business of the dream substitution . . ."

"You hit it on the head," said Farris; "that's the core of it. We'd had to fill you in before too long, so I might as well fill you in right now."

He settled back comfortably in his chair. "It started long ago, and it has been carried on with tight security for more than seven hundred years. It had to be a long-range project, you understand, for few dreams last less than a hundred years and many last much longer. At first, the work was carried on slowly and very cautiously; in those days, the men in charge had to feel their way along. But in the past few hundred years it has been safe to speed it up. We've worked through the greater part of the program first laid out, and are taking care of some of the supplementary angles that have been added since. Less than another hundred years and we'll be ready—we could be ready any time, but we'd like to wait another hundred years. We have worked up techniques from what we've already done that are plain impossible to believe. But they'll work; we have firsthand evidence that they are workable."

Blaine was cold inside, cold with the shock of disillusion. "All the years," he said.

Farris laughed. "You're right. All the years. And all the others thought that we were lily pure. We were at pains to make them think we were; such quiet people. We were quiet from the very start, while the others bunched their muscles, shouted. One by one they learned the lesson we had known from the very first—that you keep your mouth shut, that you do not show your strength. You wait until the proper time."

"The others learned, eventually. They took their lessons hard, but they finally learned the facts of politics—

too late. Even before there was a Central Union, Dreams
saw what was coming and planned. We sat quietly in
the corner and kept our hands neatly folded in our laps;
we bowed our heads a little and kept our eyes half
closed—a pose of utter meekness. Most of the time,
the others didn't even know that we were around. We
are so small and quiet, you see. Everyone is watching
Communications or Transportation or Food or Fabrication, because they are the big boys. But they should
be watching Dreams, for Dreams is the one that has it."

"Just one thing," said Blaine. "Two things, maybe.
How do you know the substitute dreams run true? All
the genuine ones we make are pure fantasy; they couldn't
really happen the way we fabricate them."

"That," Farris told him, "is the one thing that has
us on the ropes. When we can explain that one, we'll
have everything. Back at the beginning there were experiments. Dreams tried it out on their own personnel—ones
who volunteered, for short periods, five years or ten. And
the dreams didn't come out the way they were put in.

"When you give a dream a logical basis, instead of
wish-fulfillment factors, it follows the lines of logic. When
you juggle cultural factors, the patterns run true—well,
maybe not true, but different than you thought they
would. When you feed in illogic, you get a jumble of
illogic; but when you feed in logic, the logic takes over
and it shapes the dream. Our study of logic dreams
leads us to believe that they follow lines of true development. Unforeseen trends show up, governed by laws and
circumstances we could not have guessed—and those
trends work out to logical conclusions."

There was fear in the man—a fear that must have
lain deep in the minds of many men throughout seven
hundred years. "Is it just pretend? Or do those dreams
actually exist? Are there such other worlds somewhere?
And if they are, do we create them? Or do we merely
tap them?"

"How do you know about the dreams?" asked Blaine.
"The Sleepers wouldn't tell you; if they did, you couldn't
believe . . ."

Farris laughed. "That's the easy part. We have a
two-way helmet. A feed-in to establish the pattern and

to set up the factors, a sort of introduction to set the dream going. It operates for a brief period, then cuts out and the dream is on its own. But we have a feed-back built into the helmet, and the dream is put on tape. We study it as it comes in; we don't have to wait. We have stacks of tape. We have at our fingertips the billions of factors that go into many thousand different cultures. We have a history of the never-was, and of the might-have-been, and perhaps the yet-to-come."

Dreams is the one that has it, he had said. They had stacks of tape from seven hundred years of dreams. They had millions of man-hours experience—first-hand experience—in cultural patterns that had never happened; Some of them could not have happened; others of them might have come within a hair-breadth of happening— and there were many of them, perhaps, that could be made to happen.

From those tapes they had learned lessons outside the curriculum of human experience. Economics, politics, sociology, philosophy, psychology—in all facets of human effort they held all the trumps. They could pull out economic dazzlers to blind the people; they could employ political theory that would be sure to win hands down; they had psychological tricks that would stop all the other unions dead.

They played dumb for years sitting meekly in the corner, hands folded in their lap, being very quiet. And all the time they had been fashioning a weapon for use at its proper time.

And the dedication, Blaine thought, *the human dedication. The pride and comfort of a job well done. The warmth of accomplishment and service—the close human fellowship.*

For years the tapes had rolled, recording the feed-back, while men and women—who had come in trusting confidence to seek fairylands of their imagination—plodded drearily through of logic dreams that were utterly fantastic.

Farris' voice had gone on and on and now it came back to him.

". . . Giesey was going soft on us. He wanted to replace Roemer with someone who would see it his way.

And he picked you, Blaine—of all men, he picked you."

He laughed again, uproariously. "It does beat hell how mistaken one can be."

"Yes, it does," agreed Blaine.

"So we had to kill him before the appointment could go through; but you beat us to it, Blaine. You're a fast man on your feet. How did you know about it? How did you know what to do?"

"Never mind."

"The timing," said Farris. "The timing was perfect."

"You've got it all doped out."

Farris nodded. "I talked to Andrews. He'll go along; he doesn't like it, of course, but there's nothing he can do."

"You're taking a long chance, Farris, telling me all this."

"Not a chance; you are one of us. You can't get out of it. If you say a word, you wreck the guild—and you won't have a chance to say a word. From this moment, Blaine, there's a gun against your back; there'll be someone watching all the time.

"Don't try to do it, Blaine; I like you. I like the way you operate. That Education angle is pure genius. You play along with us, and it'll be worth your while. There's nothing you *can* do but play along with us; you're in it, clear up to your chin. As the head of Records, you have custody of all the evidence, and you can't write off that fact ... Go on, man; finish up that drink."

"I'd forgotten it," said Blaine.

He flicked the glass and the liquor splashed out, into Farris' face. As if it were the same motion, Blaine's fingers left the glass, let it drop, and reached for the liquor bottle.

Paul Farris came to his feet, blinded, hands clawing at his face. Blaine rose with him, bottle arcing, and his aim was good. The bottle crashed on the goon leader's skull and the man went down upon the carpeting, with snakes of blood oozing through his hair.

For a second Norman Blaine stood there. The room and the man upon the floor suddenly were bright and sharp, each feature of the place and the shape upon the carpeting burning themselves into his consciousness. He lifted his hand and saw that he still grasped the bottle's neck with its jagged, broken edges. He hurled it from him and ran, hunched against the expected bullet, straight toward the window. He leaped and rolled himself into a ball even as he leaped, arms wrapped around his face. He crashed into the glass, heard the faint *ping* of its explosion, and then was through and falling.

He lit on the gravel path and rolled until thick shrubbery stopped him, then crawled swiftly toward the wall. But the wall was smooth, he remembered—not one to be climbed. Smooth and high and with only one gate. They would hunt him down and kill him. They'd shake him out like a rabbit in a brushpile. He didn't have a chance.

He didn't have a gun and he'd not been trained to fight. All that he could do was hide and run; even so, he couldn't get away, for there wasn't much to hide in and there wasn't far to run. *But I'm glad I did it,* he told himself.

It was a blow against the shame of seven hundred years, a re-assertion of the old, dead dedication. The blow should have been struck long ago; it was useless now, except as a symbol that only Norman Blaine would know.

He wondered how much such symbolism might count in this world around him.

Blaine heard them running now, and shouting; he knew it would not be long. He huddled in the bushes and tried to plan what he should do, but everywhere he ran into blank walls and there was nothing he could do.

A voice hissed at him, a whisper from the wall. Blaine started, pressing himself further back into the clump of bushes.

"Psst," said the voice once again.

A trick, he thought, wildly. *A trick to lure me out.* Then he saw the rope, dangling from the wall, where it was lighted by the broken window.

"Psst," said the voice.

Blaine took the chance. He leaped from the bushes and across the path toward the wall. The rope was real and was anchored. Spurred by desperation, Blaine went up it like a monkey, flung out an arm across the top of the wall and hauled himself upward. A gun cracked angrily; a bullet hit the wall and ricocheted, wailing, out into the night.

Without thinking of the danger, he hurled himself off the wall. He struck hard ground that drove the breath from him and he doubled up with agony, retching, gasping to regain his breath, while stars wheeled with tortuous deliberation in the center of his brain.

He felt hands lifting him and carrying him and heard the slamming of a door, then the flow of speed as a car howled through the night.

II

A face was talking to him and Norman Blaine tried to place it; he knew that he'd seen it once before. But he couldn't recognize it; he shut his eyes, tried to find soft, cool blackness. The blackness was not soft, but harsh and painful; he opened his eyes again.

The face still was talking to him and had shoved itself up close to him. He felt the fine spray of the other's saliva fly against his face. Once before, when a man had talked to Blaine, this had happened. That morning at the parking lot a man had buttonholed him. And here he was again, with his face thrust close and the words pouring out of him.

"Cut it out, Joe," said another voice. "He's still half out. You hit him too hard; he can't understand you."

And Blaine knew that voice too. He put out his hand, pushed the face away, and hauled himself to a sitting position, with a rough wall against his back.

"Hello, Collins," he said to the second voice. "How did you get here?"

"I was brought," said Collins.

"So I heard."

Blaine wondered where he was: An old cellar, apparently—a fit place for conspirators. "Friends of yours?" he asked.

"It turns out that they are."

The face of the Buttonholer popped up once again.

"Keep him away from me," said Blaine.

Another voice told Joe to get away. And he knew that voice, too.

Joe's face left.

Blaine put up his arm and wiped his own face. "Next," he said, "I'll find Farris here."

"Farris is dead," said Collins.

"I didn't think you had the guts," said Lucinda Silone.

He turned his head against the roughness of the wall and he saw them now, standing to one side of him— Collins and Lucinda and Joe and two others that he did not know.

"He won't laugh again," said Blaine. "I smashed the laugh off him."

"Dead men never laugh," said Joe.

"I didn't hit him very hard."

"Hard enough."

"How do you know?"

"We made sure," said Lucinda.

He remembered her from the morning, sitting across the desk from him, and the calmness of her. She still was calm. She was one, Blaine thought, who could make sure—very sure—that a man was dead.

It would not have been too hard to do. Blaine had been seen going over the wall and there would have been a chase. While the guard poured out after him it would have been a fairly simple matter to slip into the house and make entirely certain that Farris was dead.

He reached up a hand and felt the lump on his head, back of the ear. They had made certain of him, too, he thought—certain that he would not wake too soon and that he'd make no trouble. He stumbled to his feet and stood shakily, putting out a hand against the wall to support himself.

He looked at Lucinda. "Education," he said, and he looked at Collins and said, "You too."

And he looked at the rest of them, from one to another. "And you?" he asked. "Every one of you?"

"Education has known it for a long time," Lucinda told him. "For a century or more. We've been working on you; and this time, my friend, we have Dreams nailed down."

"A conspiracy," said Blaine, grim laughter in his throat. "A wonderful combination—Education and conspiracy. And the Buttonholers. Oh, God, don't tell me the Buttonholers!"

She held her chin just a little tilted and her shoulders were straight. "Yes, the Buttonholers, too."

"Now," Blaine told her, "I've heard everything." He flicked a questioning thumb at Collins.

"A man," said the girl, "who took a Dream before we ever knew; who took you at the outward value that you give yourselves. We got to him . . ."

"Got to him!"

"Certainly. You don't think that we're without—well, you might call them representatives, at Center."

"Spies."

"All right; call them spies."

"And I—where do I work in? Or did I just stumble in the way?"

"You in the way? Never! You were so conscientious, dear. So smug and self-satisfied, so idealistic."

So he'd not been entirely wrong, then. It *had* been an Education plot—except that the plot had run headlong into a Center intrigue and he'd been caught in the middle. And oh the beauty of it, he thought—the utter, fouled-up beauty of it! You couldn't have worked a tangled mass like this up intentionally if you'd spent a lifetime at it.

"I told you, pal," said Collins, "that there was something wrong. That the dream was made to order for a certain purpose."

Purpose, Blaine thought. The purpose of collecting data from hypothetical civilizations, from imaginary cultures, of having first-hand knowledge as to what would happen under many possible conditions; to collect and co-ordinate that data and pick from it the factors that could be grafted onto the present culture; to go about the construction of a culture in a cold-blooded, scientific manner, as a carpenter might set out to build a hen-coop. And the lumber and the nails used in that hen-coop culture would have been fabricated from the stuff of dreams dreamt by reluctant dreamers.

And the purpose of Education in exposing the plot? Politics, perhaps. For the union which could unmask such duplicity would gain much in the way of public admiration, would thus be strengthened for the coming showdown. Or perhaps the purpose might be more idealistic, honestly motivated by a desire to thwart a scheme which would most surely put one union in unquestioned domination of all the rest of them.

"Now what?" Blaine asked.

"They want me to bring a complaint," said Collins.

"And you are going to do it."

"I suppose I shall."

"But why you? Why now? There were others with substituted dreams; you were not the first. Education must have sleepers planted by the hundreds."

He looked at the girl. "You applied," he said; "you tried to plant yourself."

"Did I?" she asked.

And had she? Or had her application been aimed at him—for now it was clear that he had been selected as one weak link in Dreams. How many other weak links now and in the past, had Education used? Had her application been a way to contact him, a means of applying some oblique pressure to make him do a thing that Education might want someone like him to do?

"We are using Collins," said Lucinda, "because he is the first independent grade A specimen we have found, who is untainted with brush of Education espionage. We used our own sleepers to build up the evidence, but we could not produce in court evidence collected by admitted spies. But Collins is clean; he took the sleep before we even suspected what was going on."

"He is not the first; there have been others. Why haven't you used them?"

"They were not available."

"Not..."

"Dreams could tell what happened. Perhaps you might know what happened to them, Mr. Blaine."

He shook his head. "But why am I here? You certainly don't expect me to testify. What made you grab me off?"

"We saved your neck," said Collins; "you keep forgetting that."

"You may leave," Lucinda told him, "any time you wish."

"Except," Joe said, "you are a hunted man. The goons are looking for you."

"If I were you," said Collins, "I do believe I'd stay."

They thought they had him. He could see they thought so—had tied and haltered, had him in a corner where he would have to do anything they said. A cold, hard anger grew inside of him—that anyone should think so easily to trap a man of Dreams and bend him to their will.

Norman Blaine took a slow step forward, away from the wall, and stood unsupported in the dim-lit cellar. "Which way out?" he asked.

"Up those steps," said Collins.

"Can you make it?" Lucinda asked.

"I can make it."

He walked unsteadily toward the stairs, but each step seemed to be a little surer and he knew he'd make it, up the stairs and out into the coolness of the night. Suddenly he yearned for the first breath of the cool, night air, to be out of this dank hole that smelled of dark conspiracy.

He turned and faced them, where they stood like big-eyed ghosts against the cellar wall. "Thanks for everything," he said.

He stood there for another instant, looking back at them. "For *everything*," he repeated.

Then he turned and climbed the stairs.

12

The night was dark, though dawn could not be far off. The moon had set, but the stars burned like steady lamps and a furtive dawn-wind had come up to skitter down the street.

He was in a little village, Blaine saw—one of the many shopping centers scattered across the countryside, with its myriad shop fronts and their glowing night lights.

He walked away from the cellar opening, lifting his head so the wind could blow against it. The air was clean and fresh after the dankness of the cellar; he gulped in great breaths of it, and it seemed to clear his head of fog and put new strength into his legs.

The street was empty; he trudged along it, wondering what he should do next. Obviously, he had to do something. The move was up to him. He couldn't be found, come morning, still wandering the streets of this shopping center.

He must find some place to hide from the hunting goons!

But there was no way in which he could hide from them. They'd be relentless in their search for Blaine. He had killed their leader—or had seemed to kill him— and that was a precedent they could not allow to go unpunished.

There'd be no public hue or outcry, for the Farris killing could not be advertised; but that would not mean the search would be carried on with any less ferocity. Even now they would be hunting for him, even now they would have covered all his likely haunts and contacts. He could not go home, or to Harriet's home, or to any of the other places—

Harriet's home!

Harriet was not home; she was off somewhere, tracking down a story that he must somehow stop. There was a greater factor here than his personal safety. There was the honor and the integrity of the Dream guild; if any of its honor and integrity were left.

But there was, Norman Blaine told himself. It still was left in the thousands of workers, and in the departmental heads who had never heard of substituted dreams. The basic purpose of the guild still remained what it had been for a thousand years, so far as the great majority of its members were concerned. To them the flame of service, the pride and comfort of that service, and the dedication to it burned as bright and clear as it ever had.

But not for long; not for many hours. The first headline in a paper, the first breath of whispered scandal, and the bright, clear light of purpose would be a smoky flare, glaring redly in the murk of shame.

There was a way—there had to be a way—to stop it.

There must be a way in which the Dream guild could be saved. And if there were a way, he must be the one to find it; of them all, Blaine was the only one who knew the imminence of dishonor.

The first step was to get hold of Harriet, to talk with her, to make her see the right and wrong.

The goons were hunting for him, but they would be on their own; they could not enlist the help of any other union. It should be safe to phone.

Far up the street, he saw a phone booth sign and he headed there, hurrying along, his footsteps ringing sharply in the morning chill.

He dialed the number of Harriet's office.

No, the voice said, she wasn't there. No, he had no idea. Should he have her call back if she happened to come in.

"Never mind," said Blaine.

He called another number.

"We're closed," a voice told him, "there's no one here at all."

He called another and there was no answer.

Another. "There ain't no one here, mister. We closed up hours ago. It's almost morning now."

She wasn't at her office; she wasn't at her favorite night spots.

Home, perhaps?

He hesitated for a moment, then decided it wasn't safe to call her there. The goons in defiance of all Communications regulations, would have her home line tapped, and his home line as well.

There was that little place out by the lake where they'd gone one afternoon. *Just a chance,* he told himself.

He looked up the number, dialed it. "Sure she's here," said the man who answered.

He waited.

"Hello, Norm," she said, and he could sense the panic in her voice the little quick catch in her breath.

"I have to talk with you."

"No," she said. "No. What do you mean by calling? You can't talk with me. The goons are hunting you ..."

"I've got to talk to you; that story ..."

"I've got the story, Norm."

"But you have to listen to me. The story's wrong. It's not the way you have it; that's not the way it was at all."

"You better get away, Norm. The goons are everywhere . . ."

"Damn the goons," he said.

"Goodbye, Norm," she said; "I hope you get away." The line was dead.

He sat stunned staring at the phone.

I hope you get away. Goodbye, Norm. I hope you get away.

She had been frightened when he'd called. She wouldn't listen; she was sorry, now, that she had ever known him— a man disgraced, a killer, hunted by the goons.

She had the story she had told him; and that was all that mattered. A story wormed out of the whispered word, out of a gin and tonic or a Scotch and soda. The old, wise story garnered from many confidences, from knowing the right people, from having many pipelines.

"Ugly," he said.

So she had the story and would write it soon and it would be splashed in garish lettering for the world to read.

There must be a way to stop it—there had to be a way to stop it.

There was a way to stop it!

He shut his eyes and shivered, suddenly cold with the horror. "No, no," he said.

But it was the only answer. Blaine got up, groped his way out of the booth, and stood in the loneliness of the empty sidewalk, with the splashes of light thrown across the concrete from the many shop fronts with the first dawn wind stirring in the sky above the roofs.

A car came creeping down the street, with its lights off, and he did not see it until it was almost opposite him. The driver stuck out his head. "Ride, mister?"

He jumped, startled by the car and the voice. His muscles bunched but there was no place to go, no place to duck, nowhere to hide. They had him cold, he knew. He wondered why they didn't shoot.

The back door popped open. "Get in here," said

Lucinda Silone. "Don't stand and argue. Get in, you crazy fool."

He moved swiftly, leaped into the car and slammed the door.

"I couldn't leave you out there naked," said the girl. "The way you are, the goons would have you before the sun was up."

"I have to go to Center," Blaine told her. "Can you take me there?"

"Of all the places . . ."

"I have to go," he said; "if you won't take me . . ."

"We can take you."

"We can't take him and you know it," said the driver.

"Joe, the man wants to go to Center."

"It's a stupid business," said Joe. "What does he want to go to Center for? We can hide him out. We . . ."

"They won't be looking for me there," said Blaine. "That's the last place in the world they'd expect to find me."

"You can't get in . . ."

"I can get him in," Lucinda said.

13

They came around a curve and were confronted by the road block. There was no time to stop, no room to turn around and flee. "Get down!" yelled Joe.

The motor howled in sudden fury at an accelerator jammed tight against the boards. Blaine reached out an arm and pulled Lucinda to him, hurling both of them off the seat and to the floor.

Metal screamed and grated as the car slammed into the block. Out of the corner of his eye, Norman Blaine saw timber go hurtling past the window. Something else smashed into a window and they were sprayed with glass.

The car bucked and slewed, then was through. One tire was flat, thumping and pounding on the pavement.

Blaine reached up a hand and grasped the back of the seat. He hauled himself up pulling Lucinda with him.

The hood of the machine, sprung loose, canted upward, blocking out the driver's vision of the road. The metal of the hood was twisted and battered, flapping in the wind. "Can't hold it long," Joe grunted, fighting the wheel.

He turned his head, a swift glance back at them, then swung it back again. Half of Joe's face, Blaine saw, was covered with blood from a cut across the temple.

A shell exploded off to one side of them. Flying, jagged metal slammed into the careening car.

Hand mortars—and the next one would be closer!

"Jump!" yelled Joe.

Blaine hesitated, and a swift thought flashed in his mind. He couldn't jump; he couldn't leave this man alone—this Buttonholer by the name of Joe. He had to stick with him. After all, this was his fight much more than it was Joe's.

Lucinda's fingers bit into his arm. "The door!"

"But Joe . . ."

"The door!" she screamed at him.

Another shell exploded, in front of the car and slightly to one side. Blaine's hand found the button of the door and pressed. The door snapped open, retracting back into the body. He hurled himself at the opening.

His shoulder slammed into concrete and he skidded along it; then the concrete ended, and he fell into nothingness. He landed in water and thick mud and fought his way up out of it, sputtering and coughing, dripping slime and muck.

His head buzzed madly and there was a dull ache in his neck. One shoulder, where he'd hit and skidded on the concrete, seemed to be on fire. He smelled the acrid odor of the muck, the mustiness of decaying vegetation, and the wind that blew down the roadside ditch was so cold it made him shiver.

Far up the road, another shell exploded, and in the flash of light he saw metallic objects flying out into the dark. Then a column of flame flared up and burned, like a lighted torch.

There went the car, he thought.

And there went Joe as well—the little man who'd waylaid him in the parking lot that morning, a little Buttonholer for whom he'd felt anger and disgust. But a man who'd died, who had been willing to die, for something that was bigger than himself.

Blaine floundered up the ditch, stooping low to keep in the cover of the reeds the grew along its edges. "Lucinda!"

There was a floundering in the water ahead. He wondered briefly at the thankfulness of relief that welled up inside of him.

She had made it, then; she was safe, here in the ditch—although to be in the ditch was only temporary safety. They might have been seen by the watching goons. They had to get away, as swiftly as they could.

The flare of the burning car was dying down and the ditch was darker now. He floundered ahead, trying to be as quiet as possible.

She was waiting for him, crouched against the bank. "All right?" he whispered and she nodded at him, her face making the quick motion in the darkness.

She lifted an arm and pointed; there, seen through the tightgrowing reeds of the marsh beyond the ditch, was Center, a great building that towered against the first light of morning in the eastern sky. "We're almost there," she told him softly.

She led the way slowly along the ditch and off into the marsh, following a watery runway that ran through the thick cover of sedges and rushes. "You know where you are going?"

"Just follow me," she told him.

He wondered vaguely how many others might have followed this hidden path across the marsh—how many times she herself might have followed it. Although it was hard to think of her as she was now, dirty with muck and slime, wading through the water. Behind them they still could hear the shouts of the squad of goons that had been stationed at the block.

The goons had gone all out, he thought, setting up a block on a public highway. Someone could get into a lot of trouble for a stunt like that.

He'd told Lucinda that the goons would never dream of his going back to Center. But he had been wrong; apparently they had expected he'd try to make it back to Center. And they'd been set and waiting for him. Why?

Lucinda had halted in front of the mouth of a three-foot drain pipe, emerging from the bank just above the waterway. A tiny trickle of water ran out of it and dripped into the swamp. "How are you at crawling?"

"I can do anything," he told her.

"It's a long ways."

He glanced up at the massive Center which, from where he stood, seemed to rise out of the marsh. "All the way?"

"All the way," she said.

She lifted a muddy hand and brushed back a strand of hair, leaving a streak of mud across her face. He grinned at the sight of her—sodden and bedraggled, no longer the cool, unruffled creature who had sat across the desk from him. "If you laugh out loud," she said, "I swear I'll smack you one."

She braced her elbows on the lip of the pipe and hauled herself upward, wriggling into the pipe. She gained the pipe and went forward on hands and knees.

Blaine followed. "You know your way around," he whispered, the pipe catching up the whisper and magnifying it, bouncing it back and forth in an eerie echo.

"We had to, we fought a vicious enemy."

They crawled and crept in silence, then, for what seemed half of eternity. "Here," said Lucinda. "Careful."

She reached back a hand and guided him forward in the darkness. A glow of feeble light came from a break in the side of the pipe, where a chunk of the tile had been broken or had fallen out. "Tight squeeze," she told him.

He watched her wriggle through and drop from sight. Blaine followed cautiously. A broken spear of the tile bit into his back and ripped his shirt, but he forced his body through and dropped.

They stood in a dim-lit corridor. The air smelled foul and old; the stones dripped with dampness. They came to stairs and climbed them, went along another corridor for a ways, then climbed again.

Then, suddenly, there were no dripping stones and dankness, but a familiar hall of marble, with the first-floor murals shining on the walls above the gleaming bronze of elevator doors.

There were robots in the hall; suddenly, the robots all were looking at them and starting to walk toward them.

Lucinda backed against the wall.

Blaine grabbed at her wrist.

"Quick," he said. "Back the way . . ."

"Blaine," said one of the advancing robots. "Wait a minute, Blaine."

He swung around and waited. All the robots stopped. "We've been waiting for you," said the robot spokesman. "We were sure you'd make it."

Blaine jerked at Lucinda's wrist. "Wait," she whispered. "There's something going on here."

"Roemer said you would come back," the robot said. "He said that you would try."

"Roemer? What has Roemer got to do with it?"

"We are with you," said the robot. "We threw out all the goons. Please allow me, sir."

The doors of the nearest elevator were slowly sliding back.

"Let's go along," Lucinda said. "It sounds all right to me."

They stepped into the elevator, with the robot spokesman following.

The car shot up and stopped. The door opened and they stepped out, between two solid lines of robots, flanking their path from the elevator to the door marked Records.

A man stood in the door, a great foursquare, dark-haired man whom Norman Blaine had seen before on a few occasions. A man who had written: *If you should want to see me later, I am at your service.*

"I heard about it, Blaine," said Roemer. "I hoped you'd try to make it back; I figured you were that kind of man."

Blaine stared back at him haggardly. "I'm glad you think so, Roemer. Five minutes from now . . ."

"It had to be someone," said Roemer. "Don't think about it too much. It simply had to come."

Blaine walked on leaden feet between the file of robots, brushed past Roemer at the door.

The phone was on the desk and Norman Blaine lowered himself into the chair before it. Slowly he reached out his hand.

No! No! There must be another way. There must be another, better way to beat them—Harriet with her story; and the goons who were hunting him; and the plot with its roots reaching back through seven hundred years. Now he could make it stick—with Roemer and the robots he could make it stick. When he'd first thought of it, he had not been sure he could. His only thought then, he remembered, had been to get back to Center somehow, to get into this office and try to hold the place long enough, so he could not be stopped from doing what he meant to do.

He had expected to die here, behind some desk or chair, with a goon bullet in his body, and a shattered door through which the goons had finally burst their way.

There had to be another way—but there was no other way. There was only one way—the bitter fruit of seven hundred years of sitting quietly in the corner, with hands folded in one's lap, and poison in one's brain. He lifted the receiver out of the cradle and held it there, looking across the desk at Roemer.

"How did you do it?" he asked. "These robots? Why did you do it, John?"

"Giesey's dead," said Roemer; "so is Farris. No one has been appointed to their posts. Chain of command, my friend. Business agent, Protection, Records—you're the big boss now; you've been the head of Dreams since the moment Farris died."

"Oh, my God," said Blaine.

"The robots are loyal," Roemer went on. "Not to any man; not to any one department. They are conditioned to be loyal to Dreams. And you, my friend, are Dreams. For how long, I don't know; but at the moment you are Dreams."

They stared at one another for a long moment.

"The authority is yours," said Roemer; "go ahead and make your call."

So that was why, Blaine thought, *the goons assumed I would return.* That was why they'd set up the road block, not on one road only, perhaps, but on all of them—so that he could not get back and take over before someone could be named.

I should have thought of it, he told himself. *I knew it. I thought of it this very afternoon, how I was third in line—*

The operator was saying: "Number, please. Number, please. What number do you wish please."

Blaine gave the number and waited.

Lucinda had laughed at him and said: "You are a dedicated man." Perhaps not those words exactly but that had been what she meant. Mocking him with his dedication; prodding him to see what he would do. A dedicated man, she'd said. And now, here finally, was the price of dedication.

"News" said a voice. "This is Central News."

"I have a story for you."

"Who is speaking, please?"

"Norman Blaine. I am Blaine, of Dreams."

"Blaine?" A pause. "You said your name was Blaine?"

"That's right."

"We have a story here," said Central News, "from one of our branches. We've been checking it. We held it up, in fact, to check it . . ."

"Put me on the transcription. I want you to get this right; I don't want to be misquoted."

"You're on transcription sir."

"Then here you are . . ."

Then here you are.

Here is the end of it—

"Go ahead, Blaine."

Blaine said, "Here it is, then. For seven hundred years, the Dreams guild has been carrying out a series of experiments aimed at the study of parallel cultures . . ."

"That is what the story we have says, sir; you are sure that that is right?"

"You disbelieve it?"

"No, but . . ."

"It's true. We've worked on it for seven hundred years —under strict security because of certain continuing situations which made it seem unwise to say anything about it . . ."

"The story I have here . . ."

"Forget the story that you have!" Blaine shouted. "I don't know what it's all about; I called you up to tell you that we're giving it away. Do you understand that? *We're giving it away.* Within the next few days, we plan to make all our data available to a commission we'll ask to be set up. Its membership will be chosen from the various unions, to assess the data and decide where use may best be made of it."

"Blaine. Wait a minute, Blaine."

Roemer reached out for the phone. "Let me finish it; you're beat out. Take it easy now. I will handle it."

He lifted the receiver, smiling. "They'll want your authority, and all the rest of it."

He smiled again. "This was what Giesey wanted, Blaine. That's why Farris made him fire me; that's why Farris killed him . . ."

Roemer spoke into the phone. "Hello, sir. Blaine had to leave; I'll fill in the rest . . ."

The rest? There wasn't any more. Couldn't they understand? He'd make it very simple.

Dreams was giving up its one last chance at greatness. It was all Dreams had, and Norman Blaine had given it away. He had beaten Harriet and Farris and the hunting goons, but it was a bitter, empty victory.

It saved the pride of Dreams; and that was all it saved.

Something—some thought, some impulse, made him lift his head, almost as if someone had called to him from across the room.

Lucinda stood beside the door, looking at him, with a gentle smile upon her mud-streaked face, and her eyes were deep and soft. "Can't you hear them cheering?" she asked. "Can't you hear the whole world cheering you? It's been a long time, Norman Blaine, since the whole world cheered together!"

THE SPACEMAN'S VAN GOGH

THE PLANET was so unimportant and so far out toward the rim that it didn't have a name, but just a code and number as a key to its position. The village had a name, but one that was impossible for a human to pronounce correctly.

It cost a lot to get there. Well, not to get there, exactly, for all one did was *polt* there; but it cost a hunk of cash to have the co-ordinates set up for the *polting*. Because the planet was so far away, the computer had to do a top-notch job, correct to seven decimal points. Otherwise one took the chance of materializing a million miles off desti-nation, in the depths of space; or if you hit the planet, a thousand or so miles up; or worse yet, a couple hundred underneath the surface. Any one of which would be highly inconvenient, if not positively fatal.

There was no reason in the universe for anyone to go there—except Anson Lathrop. Lathrop had to go there because it was the place where Reuben Clay had died.

So he paid out a pocketful of cash to get himself indoc-trinated to the planet's mores and speech, and a bucketful of cash to get his *polting* plotted—a two-way job, to get both there and back.

He arrived there just about midday, not at the village exactly, for even seven decimal points weren't good enough to land him squarely in it—but not more than twenty miles away, as it turned out, and no more than twelve feet off the ground.

He picked himself up and dusted himself off and was thankful for the knapsack that he wore, for he had landed on it and been cushioned from the fall.

The planet, or what he could see of it, was a dismal place. It was a cloudy day and he had trouble making out, so colorless was the land, where the horizon ended and the sky began. The ground was flat, a great plain unrelieved by trees or ridge, and covered here and there by patches of low brush.

He had landed near a path and in this he considered himself lucky, for he remembered from his indoctrination that the planet had no roads and not too many paths.

He hoisted his knapsack firmly into place and started down the path. In a mile or so he came to a signpost, badly weather-beaten, and while he wasn't too sure of the symbols, it seemed to indicate he was headed in the wrong direction. So he turned back, hoping fervently he had read the sign correctly.

He arrived at the village just as dusk was setting in, after a lonely hike during which he met no one except a strange and rather ferocious animal which sat erect to watch him pass, whistling at him all the while as if it were astounded at him.

Nor did he see much more when he reached the village.

The village, as he had known it would, resembled nothing quite so much as one of the prairie dog towns which one could see in the western part of North America, back on his native Earth.

At the edge of the village he encountered plots of cultivated ground with strange crops growing in them; and working among some of these plots in the gathering darkness were little gnome-like figures. When he stopped and called to them, they merely stared at him for a moment and then went back to work.

He walked down the village's single street, which was little more than a well-travelled path, and tried to make some sense out of the entrances to the burrows, each of which was backed by a tumulus of the ground dug up in its excavation. Each mound looked almost exactly like every other mound and no burrow mouth seemed to have anything to distinguish it from any of the others.

Before some of the burrows tiny gnome-like figures played—children, he supposed—but at his approach they scuttled rapidly inside and did not reappear.

He travelled the entire length of the street; and standing there, he saw what he took to be a somewhat larger mound, some little distance off, surmounted by what appeared to be some sort of rude monument, a stubby spire that pointed upward like an accusing finger aimed toward the sky.

And that was a bit surprising, for there had been no mention in his indoctrination—of monuments or of religious structures. Although, he realized, his indoctrination would be necessarily skimpy for a place like this; there was not a great deal known of the planet or its people.

Still, it might not be unreasonable to suppose that these gnomes might possess religion; here and there one still found patches of it. Sometimes it would be indigenous to the planet, and in other cases it would be survival transplantations from the planet Earth or from one of the other several systems where great religions once had flourished.

He turned around and went back down the street again and came to a halt in the middle of the village. No one came out to meet him, so he sat down in the middle of the path and waited. He took a lunch out of his knapsack, ate it, and drank water out of the vacuum bottle that he carried, and wondered why Reuben Clay had picked this dismal place in which to spend his final days.

Not that it would be out of keeping with the man. It was a humble place and Clay had been a humble man, known as the "Spaceman's Van Gogh" at one time. He had lived within himself rather than with the universe which surrounded him. He had not sought glory or acclaim, although he could have claimed them both—at times, indeed, it appeared that he might be running from them. Throughout his entire life there had been the sense of a man who hid away. Of a man who ran from something, or a man who ran after something—a seeking, searching man who never quite caught up with the thing he sought for. Lathrop shook his head. It was hard to know which sort Clay had been—a hunted man or hunter. If hunted, what had it been he feared? And if a hunter, what could it be he sought?

Lathrop heard a light scuffing in the path and turned his head to see that one of the gnome-like creatures was approaching him. The gnome was old, he saw. Its fur was gray and grizzled and when it came closer he saw the other marks of age upon it—the rheumy eyes, the wrinkled skin, the cragged bushiness of its eyebrows, the cramped stiffness of its hands.

It stopped and spoke to him and he puzzled out the language.

"Good seeing to you, sir." Not "sir," of course, but the nearest translation one could make.

"Good hearing," Lathrop said ceremoniously.

"Good sleeping."

"Good eating," Lathrop said.

Finally they both ran out of "goods."

The gnome stood in the path and had another long look at him. Then: "You are like the other one."

"Clay," said Lathrop.

"Younger," said the gnome.

"Younger," Lathrop admitted. "Not much younger."

"Just right," said the gnome, meaning it to be a diplomatic compliment.

"Thank you."

"Not sick."

"Healthy," Lathrop said.

"Clay was sick. Clay ......" Not "died." More like "discontinued" or possibly "ended," but the meaning was clear.

"I know that. I came to talk about him."

"Lived with us," said the gnome. "He (die?) with us."

How long ago? How did you ask how long? There was, Lathrop realized with something of a shock, no gnome-words for duration or measurement of time. A past, present and future tense, of course, but no word for measurement of either time or space.

"You . . . ." There was no word for *buried*. No word for *grave*.

"You planted him?" asked Lathrop.

He sensed the horror that his question raised. "We. . . . him."

Ate him? Lathrop wondered. Some of the ancient tribes of Earth and on other planets, too, ate their dead, thereby conferring tender honors on them.

But it was not eat.

Burned? Scaffolded? Exposed?

No, it was none of those.

"We . . . . him," the gnome insisted. "It was his wish. We loved him. We could do no less."

Lathrop bowed gratefully. "I am honored that you did."

That seemed to mollify the gnome.

"He was a harmless one," said the gnome. Not exactly "harmless." Kind, perhaps. Uncruel. With certain connotations of soft-wittedness. Which was natural, of course, for in his nonconformity through lack of understanding, any alien must appear slightly soft-witted to another people.

As if he might have known what Lathrop was thinking, the gnome said, "We did not understand him. He had what he called a *brushandpaints*. He made streaks with them."

Streaks?

Brushandpaints? Sure, brush and paints.

Streaks? of course. For the people of this planet were colorblind. To them Clay's painting would be streaks.

"He did that here?"

"Yes. It here."

"I wonder. Might I see it?"

"Certainly," said the gnome. "If you follow me."

They crossed the street and approached a burrow's mouth. Stooping, Lathrop followed down the tunnel. Ten or twelve feet down it became a room, a sort of earthen cave.

There was a light of a sort. Not too good a light, a soft, dim light that came from little heaps of glowing material piled in crude clay dishes placed about the burrow.

Foxfire, thought Lathrop. The phosphorescent light of rotting wood.

"There," said the gnome.

The painting leaned against one wall of the burrow, an alien square of color in this outlandish place. Under ordinary circumstances, the faint foxfire light would have been too feeble for one to see the painting, but the brush strokes on the canvas seemed to have a faint light of their own, so that the colors stood out like another world glimpsed through a window beyond the foxfire dimness.

As Lathrop looked at the propped-up square, the glowing quality seemed to become more pronounced, until the picture was quite clear in all its unfinished detail—and it was not a glow, Lathrop thought; it was a *shiningness*.

And it was Clay. The painting, unfinished as it was, could not be mistaken. Even if one had not known that Clay had spent the last days of his life within this village, he still would have known that the work was Clay's. The clean outline was there, the authority of craftsmanship combined with the restrained quality, the masterly understatement, the careful detail and the keen sharp color. But there was something else as well—a certain happiness, a humble happiness that had no hint of triumph.

"He did not finish it," said Lathrop. "He did not have the . . . (there was no word for time). He (discontinued) before he finished it."

"His *brushandpaints* discontinued. He sat and looked at it."

So that was it. That was how it happened. Clay's paints had given out and there had been no place, no way—perhaps no time—in which he could have gotten more.

So Reuben Clay had sat in this burrow and looked at his last painting, knowing it was the last painting he would ever do, propped there against the wall, and had known the hopelessness of ever finishing the great canvas he had started. Although more than likely Clay had never thought of it as great. His paintings, for him, had never been more than an expression of himself. To him they had been something that lay inside himself waiting to be transferred into some expression that the universe could see, a sort of artistic communication from Clay to all his fellow creatures.

"Rest yourself," said the gnome. "You are tired."

"Thanks," said Lathrop.

He sat down on the hard-packed floor, with his back against the wall, opposite the painting.

"You knew him," said the gnome.

Lathrop shook his head.

"But you came seeking him."

"I sought word of him."

How could one, he wondered, explain to the little gnome what he sought in Clay, or why he'd tracked him down when all the universe forgot? How could one explain to these people, who were colorblind and more than likely had no conception of what a painting was—how could one explain the greatness that was Clay's? The technique that lived within his hands, the clean, quick sense of color, the almost unworldly ability to see a certain thing exactly as it was.

To see the truth and to reproduce that truth—not as a single facet of the truth, but the entire truth in its right perspective and its precise color, and with its meaning and its mood pinpointed so precisely that one need but look to know.

That may have been why I sought him, thought Lathrop. That may be why I've spent twenty Earth years and a barrel of money to learn all the facts of him. The monograph I some day will write on him is no more than a faint attempt to rationalize my search for facts—the logic that is needed to justify a thing. But it was the truth, thought Lathrop. That's the final answer of what I sought in Clay—the truth that lay in him and in his painting. Because I, too, at one time worked in truth.

"It is magic," said the gnome, staring at the painting.

"Of a sort," said Lathrop. And that probably had been why, at first, they had accepted Clay, in the expectation that some of his magic might rub off on them. But not entirely, perhaps; certainly not toward the end. For Clay was not the sort of simple, unassuming man these simple creatures would respect and love.

They'd let him live among them, more than likely finally as one of them, probably without the thought of payment for his living space and food. He may have worked a little in the fields and he may have puttered up things, but he would have been essentially their guest, for no alien creature could fit himself economically into such a simple culture.

They had helped him through his final days and watched him in his dying and when he had finally died they'd done to him a certain act of high respect and honor.

What was that word again? He could not remember it. The indoctrination had been inadequate; there were word gaps and blank spaces and blind spots and that was wholly understandable in a place like this.

He saw the gnome was waiting for him to explain the magic, to explain it better than Clay had been able to explain it. Or maybe Clay had not attempted to explain, for they might not have asked him.

The gnome waited and hoped and that was all, for he could not ask. You do not ask another race about the details of their magic.

"It is a ... (no word for representation, no word for picture) ... place that Clay saw. He tried to bring it back to life. He tried to tell you and I what he had seen. He tried to make us see it, too."

"Magic," said the gnome.

Lathrop gave up. It was impossible. To the gnome it was simple magic. So be it—simple magic.

It was a valley with a brook that gurgled somberly and with massive trees and a deep wash of light that was more than sunlight lay over all of it. There was no living creature in it and that was typical, for Clay was a landscape artist without the need of people or of other creatures.

A happy place, thought Lathrop, but a solemn happiness. A place to run and laugh, but not to run too swiftly nor to laugh too loudly, for there was a lordly reverence implicit in the composition.

"He saw many places," Lathrop told the gnome. "He put many places on a (no word for canvas or board or plane) ... on a flat like that. Many different planets. He tried to catch the ... (no word for spirit) ... the way that each planet looked."

"Magic," said the gnome. "His was powerful magic."

The gnome moved to the far wall of the room and poked up a peat fire in a primitive stove fashioned out of mud. "You are hungry," said the gnome.

"I ate."

"You must eat with us. The others will be coming. It is too dark to work."

"I will eat with you," said Lathrop.

For he must break the bread with them. He must be one of them if he were to carry out his mission. Perhaps not one of them as Clay had been one of them, but at least accepted. No matter what horrendous and disgusting thing should comprise the menu, he must eat with them.

But it was more than likely that the food would not be

too bad. Roots and vegetables, for they had gardens. Pickled insects, maybe, and perhaps some alcoholic concoction he'd have to be a little careful with.

But no matter what it was, he would have to eat with them and sleep with them and be as friendly and as thoughtful as Clay had been thoughtful and friendly.

For they'd have things to tell him, data that he'd given up all hope of getting, the story of the final days of Reuben Clay. Perhaps even some clue to the mystifying "lost years," the years when Clay had dropped completely out of sight.

He sat quietly, thinking of how the trail had come to an end, out near the edge of the galaxy, not too many light-years from this very place. For year on absorbing year he had followed Clay's trail from star to star, gathering data on the man, talking with those who'd known him, tracking down one by one the paintings he had made. And then the trail had ended. Clay had left a certain planet and no one knew where he'd gone; for years Lathrop had searched for some hint to where he'd gone, and had been close to giving up when he finally had found evidence that Clay had come to this place to die. But the evidence had strongly indicated that he had not come here directly from where the trail had stopped, but had spent several years at some other place. So there was still a gap in the story that he followed—a gap of lost years, how many years there was no way of knowing.

Perhaps here, in this village, he might get a clue to where Clay had spent those years. But, he told himself it could be no more than a clue. It could not be specific, for these little creatures had no concept of time or otherwhere.

More than likely the painting here in this burrow was in itself a clue. More than likely it was a painting of that unknown place Clay had visited before coming here to die. But if that were so, thought Lathrop, it was a slender hope, for one might spend three lifetimes—or more—combing planet after planet in the vain hope of recognizing the scene Clay had spread upon the canvas.

He watched the gnome busy at the stove, and there was no sound except the lonely whining of the wind in the chimney and at the tunnel's mouth. Lonely wind and empty moor and the little villages of heaped earth, here at the far edge of the galaxy, out in the rim of the mighty wheel of suns. How much do we know of it, he thought, this thing we call our galaxy, this blob of matter hurled out into the gulf of space by some mighty Fist? We do not know the beginning of it nor the end of it nor the reason for its being; we are blind creatures groping in the darkness for realities and the few realities we find we know as a blind man knows the things within his room, knowing them by the sense of touch alone. For in the larger sense we all are as blind as he—all of us together, all the creatures living in the galaxy. And presumptuous and precocious despite our stumbling blindness, for before we know the galaxy we must know ourselves.

We do not understand ourselves, have no idea of the purpose of us. We have tried devices to explain ourselves, materialistic devices and spiritualistic devices and the application of pure logic, which was far from pure. And we have fooled ourselves, thought Lathrop. That is mostly what we've done. We have laughed at things we do not understand, substituting laughter for knowledge, using laughter as a shield against our ignorance, as a drug to still our sense of panic. Once we sought comfort in mysticism, fighting tooth and nail against the explanation of the mysticism, for only so long as it remained mysticism and unexplained could it comfort us. We once subscribed to faith and fought to keep the faith from becoming fact, because in our twisted thinking faith was stronger than the fact.

And are we any better now, he wondered, for having banished faith and mysticism, sending the old faiths and the old religions scurrying into hiding places against the snickers of a galaxy that believes in logic and pins its hope on nothing less than fact. A step, he thought—it is but a step, this advancement to the logic and the fact, this fetish for explaining. Some day, far distant, we may find another fact that will allow us to keep the logic and the fact, but will supply once again the comfort that we lost with faith.

The gnome had started cooking and it had a good smell to it. Almost an Earth smell. Maybe, after all, the eating would not be as bad as he had feared.

"You like Clay?" the gnome asked.

"Liked him. Sure, I liked him."

"No. No. You do like he? You make the streaks like he?"

Lathrop shook his head. "I do nothing now. I am (how did you say retired?). . . . My work is ended. Now I play (play, because there was no other word)."

"Play?"

"I work no more. I do now as I please. I learn of Clay's life and I (no word for write) . . . I tell his life in streaks. Not those kind of streaks. Not the kind of streaks he made. A different kind of streaks."

When he had sat down he'd put his knapsack beside him. Now he drew it to his lap and opened it. He took out the pad of paper and a pencil. "This kind of streaks," he said.

The gnome crossed the room to stand beside him.

Lathrop wrote on his pad: *I was a whitherer. I used facts and logic to learn whither are we going. I was a seeker of truth.*

"Those kind of streaks," he said. "I have made many streaks of Clay's life."

"Magic," said the gnome.

It was all down, thought Lathrop, all that he had learned of Clay. All but the missing years. All down in page after page of notes, waiting for the writing. Notes telling the strange story of a strange man who had wandered star to star, painting planet after planet, leaving his paintings strewn across the galaxy. A man who had wandered as if he might be seeking something other than new scenes to put upon his canvases. As if his canvases were no more than a passing whim, no more than a quaint and convenient device to earn the little money that he needed for food and *polting* plots, the money that enabled him to go on to system after system. Making no effort to retain any of his work, selling every bit of it or even, at times, simply walking off and leaving it behind.

Not that his paintings weren't good. They were—startlingly good. They were given honored places in many galleries, or what passed as galleries, on many different planets.

Clay had stayed for long at no place. He had always

hurried on. As if there were a purpose or a plot which drove him from star to star.

And the sum total of the wandering, of the driven purpose, had ended here in this very burrow, no more than a hiding place against the wind and weather.

"Why?" asked the gnome. "Why make the streaks of Clay?"

"Why?" said Lathrop. "Why? I do not know!"

But the answer, not only of Clay's wandering, but of his following in Clay's tracks, might be within his grasp. Finally, after all the years of searching, he might find the answer here.

"Why do you streak?"

And how to answer that?

How had Clay answered? For they must have asked him, too. Not how, because you do not ask the how of magic. But why . . . that was permissable. Not the secret of the magic, but the purpose of it.

"So we may know," said Lathrop, groping for the words, "So all of us may know, you and I and all the others on other stars may know what kind of being (man?) Clay was."

"He was . . . . (kind?). He was one of us. We loved him. That is all we need to know."

"All you may need," said Lathrop. "But not enough for others."

Although there probably would not be many who would read the monograph once he had written it. Only a pitiful few would take the time to read it, or even care to read it.

He thought: Now, finally, I know what I've known all along, but refused to admit I knew; that I'm not doing this for others, but for myself alone. And not for the sake of occupation, not for the sake of keeping busy in retirement, but for some deeper reason and for some greater need. For some factor or some sense, perhaps, that I missed before. For some need I do not even recognize. For some purpose that might astound me if I ever understood it.

The gnome went back to the stove and got on with the meal and Lathrop continued to sit with his back against the wall, realizing now the tiredness that was in him. He'd had a busy day. *Polting* was not difficult, actually seemed easy, but it took a lot out of a man. And, in addition to that, he'd walked twenty miles from his landing place to reach the village.

Polting might be easy, but it had not been easy to come by, for its development had been forced to wait upon the suspension of erroneous belief, had come only with the end of certain superstitions and the false screen of the prejudice set up to shield Man against his lack of knowledge. For if a man did not understand a thing, he called it a silly superstition and let it go at that. The human race could disregard a silly superstition and be quite easy in its mind, but it could not disregard a stubborn fact without a sense of guilt.

Shuffling footsteps came down the tunnel and four gnomes emerged into the burrow. They carried crude gardening tools and these they set against the wall, then stood silently in a row to stare at the man sitting on the floor.

The old gnome said: "It is another one like Clay. He will stay with us."

They moved forward, the four of them, and stood in a semi-circle facing Lathrop. One of them asked the old gnome at the stove: "Will he stay here and die?" And another one said, "He is not close to dying, this one." There was anticipation in them.

"I will not die here," said Lathrop, uneasily.

"We will . . . . ," said one of them, repeating that word which told what they had done with Clay when he had died, and he said it almost as if it were a bribe to make the human want to stay and die.

"Perhaps he would not want us to," said another one. "Clay wanted us to do it. He may not feel like Clay."

There was horror in the burrow, a faint, flesh-creeping horror in the words they said and in the way they looked at him with anticipation.

The old gnome went to one corner of the burrow and came back with a bag. He set it down in front of Lathrop and tugged at the string which tied it, while all the others watched. And one could see that they watched with reverence and hope and that the opening of the bag was a great occasion—and that if there could be anything approaching solemnity in their squat bodies, they watched most solemnly.

The string finally came loose and the old gnome tilted the bag and grasped it by its bottom and emptied it upon the earthen floor. There were brushes and many tubes of paint, all but a few squeezed dry and a battered wallet and something else that the old gnome picked up from the floor and handed to the Earthman.

Lathrop stretched out his hand and took it and held it and looked at it and suddenly he knew what they had done to Clay, knew without question that great and final honor.

Laughter gurgled in his throat—not laughter at the humor of it, for there was no humor, but laughter at the twisted values, at the cross-purposes of concepts, at wondering how, and knowing how the gnomes might have arrived at the conclusion which they reached in rendering to Clay the great and final honor.

He could see it even now as it might have happened—how they worked for days carrying the earth to make the mound he'd seen beyond the village, knowing that the end was nearing for this alien friend of theirs; how they must have searched far for timber in this land of little bushes, and having found it, brought it in upon many bended backs, since they did not know the wheel; and how they fitted it together, fumblingly, perhaps, with wooden pegs and laboriously bored-out holes, for they had no metal and they knew no carpentry.

And they did it all for the love that they bore Clay, and all their labor and their time had been as nothing in the glory of this thing they did so lovingly.

He looked at the crucifix and now it seemed that he understood what had seemed so strange of Clay—the eternal searching, the mad, feverish wandering from one star system to another, even in part, the superb artistry that spoke so clearly of a hidden, half-guessed truth behind the many truths he'd spoken with his brush.

For Clay had been a survival-member of that strange, gentle sect out of Earth's far antiquity; he had been one of those who, in this world of logic and of fact, had clung to the mysticism and the faith. Although for Clay, perhaps, the naked faith alone had not been enough, even as for him, Anson Lathrop, bare facts at times seemed not enough. And that he had never guessed this truth of Clay was easy to explain—one did not fling one's faith into the gigantic snicker of a Logic universe.

For both of them, perhaps, neither fact nor faith could stand alone, but each must have some leavening of the other.

Although that is wrong, Lathrop told himself. I do not need the faith. I worked for years with logic and with fact and that is all one needs. If there is other need, it lies in another as-yet-undiscovered fact or; we need not go back to faith.

Strip the faith and the mumbo-jumbo from the fact and you have something you can use. As Man long ago had stripped the disbelief and laughter from the poltergeist and had come up with the principle of *polting,* the fact and principle that moved a man from star to star as easily as in the ancient days he might walk down the street to his favorite bar.

Yet there could be no doubt that for Clay it had not worked that way, that with fact alone he could not have painted as he did, that it took the simple faith and the inner glow of that simple faith to give him the warmth and the dedication to make his paintings what they were.

And it had been the faith that had sent him on his search throughout the galaxy.

Lathrop looked at the painting and saw the simplicity and the dignity, the tenderness and the happiness and the sense of flooding light.

Exactly the kind of light, thought Lathrop, that had been so crudely drawn in the illustrations of those old books he had studied in his course on Earth's comparative religions. There had been, he remembered, one instructor who'd spent some time on the symbolism of the light.

He dropped the crucifix and put out his hand and picked up some of the twisted tubes of oils.

The painting was unfinished, the gnome had said, because Clay had run out of paint, and there was truth in that, for the tubes were flattened and rolled up hard against the caps and one could see the imprint of the fingers that had applied the pressure to squeeze out the last drop of the precious oils.

He fled across the galaxy, thought Lathrop, *and I tracked him down.*

Even after he was dead I went on and tracked him down, sniffing along the cold trail he had left among the stars. And I tracked him because I loved him, not the man himself—for I did not know nor have any way to know what kind of man he was—but because I saw within has paintings something that all the critics missed. Something that called out to me. Deny it as I may, it may have been the ancient faith calling out to me. The faith that is missing now. The simple faith that long ago was killed by simple logic.

But he knew Clay now, Lathrop told himself. He knew him by the virtue of the tiny crucifix and by the symbol of the last great canvas and by the crude actuality of the mound that stood at the village end on this third rate planet.

And he knew why it had to be a third rate planet.

For there must be humility—even as in faith there had been humility, as there had never been in logic.

Lathrop could shut his eyes and see it—the somber clouds and the vast dreariness of the wastelands, the moors that swept on to foreverness, and the white figure on the cross and the crowd that stood beneath it, staring up at it, marked for all time by a thing they did not understand, a thing they could not understand, but a thing they had done out of utter kindness for one whose faith had touched them.

"Did he ever tell you," he asked the gnomes, "where he had been? Where he came from? Where he had been just before he came here."

They shook their heads at Lathrop. "He did not tell," they said.

Somewhere, thought Lathrop, where the trees grow like those trees in the painting. Where there was peace and dignity and tenderness—and the light.

Man had stripped the husk of superstition from the poltergeist and had found a kernel in the *polting* principle. Man had done the same with anti-gravity, and with telepathy, and many other things but he had not tried to strip the husks from faith to find the hidden kernel. For faith did not submit to investigation. Faith stood sufficient to itself and did not admit of fact.

What was faith and what the goal of faith? In the many tongues of ancient Earth, what had been the goal of those who subscribed to faith? Happy hunting ground, valhalla, heaven, the islands of the blest—how much faith, how much could be fact? One would not know unless he lived by faith alone and no being now, or very few, lived entirely by their faith.

But might there not be, in the last great reckoning of galactic life and knowledge another principle which would prove greater than either faith or fact—a principle as yet unknown, but only to be gained by aeons of intellectual evolution. Had Clay stumbled on that principle, a man who sought far ahead of time, who ran away from evolutionary knowledge and who, by that very virtue, would have grasped no more than a dim impression of the principle-to-come.

Faith had failed because it had been blinded by the shining glory of itself. Could fact as well have failed by the hard glitter of its being?

But abandoning both faith and fact, armed with a greater tool of discernment, might a man not seek and find the eventual glory and the goal for which life has grasped, knowing and unknowing, from the first faint stir of consciousness upon the myriad solar systems?

Lathrop found the tube of white and unscrewed the cap and squeezed the tube and a bit of oil came out, a tiny drop of oil. He held the tube steady in one hand and picked up a brush. Carefully he transferred the color to the brush.

He dropped the tube and walked across the burrow to the painting and squatted down and squinted at it in the feeble light, trying to make out the source of the flood of light.

Up in the left hand corner, just above the horizon, although he couldn't be entirely sure that he was right.

He extended the brush, then drew it back.

Yes, that must be it. A man would stand beneath the massive trees and face toward the light.

Careful now, he thought. Very, very careful. Just a

faint suggestion, for it was mere symbolism. Just a hint of color. One stroke perpendicular and a shorter one at right angle, closer to the top.

The brush was awkward in his hand.

It touched the canvas and he pulled it back again.

It was a silly thing, he thought. A silly thing and crazy. And, besides, he couldn't do it. He didn't know how to do it. Even at his lightest touch, it would be crude and wrong. It would be desecration.

He let the brush drop from his fingers and watched it roll along the floor.

I tried, he said to Clay.

FULL CYCLE

I

THE LETTER sent the life of Amby Wilson crashing decorously down about his ears. It was a form affair, with the address typed in with a newer, blacker ribbon; it said:

Dr. Ambrose Wilson,
Department of History
It is with regret that I must inform you the board of regents at their meeting this morning decided the university will cease to function at the end of the present term.

Contributing to the decision were the lack of funds and the progressive dwindling of the student body. You, of course, have been aware of the situation for some time, but nevertheless . . .

There was more of it, but Amby didn't read it. What still was left unread, he knew, would be no more than the grossest of platitudes.

It had been bound to happen.

The regents had hung on in the face of monstrous difficulties; the university was virtually deserted. The place that once had rung with life and pulsed with learning was now no better than a ghost school.

As the city was a ghost city.

And I a ghost; thought Amby.

He made an admission to himself, an admission he would not have made a day or hour ago: For thirty years or more he had lived in an unreal and unsubstantial world, clinging to the old, vague way of life as he first had known it. And to make that vague life the more substantial, he

94

had banished to an intellectual outer limbo any valid consideration of the world beyond the city.

And good reason that he should, he thought; good and valid reason. What was outside the city had no link with this world of his. A nomad population—an almost alien people, who had built a neo-culture rich in decadence, concocted half of provincialism, half of old folk-tales.

There was nothing there, he thought, of any value to a man like him, nothing worth the consideration of a man like him. Here in this university he had kept alight a feeble glow of the old learning and the old tradition; now the light had flickered out and the learning and tradition would go down into the darkness.

And that, he knew, was no attitude for a historian to take; history was the truth and the seeking after truth. To gloss over, to ignore, to push away an eventful fact—no matter how distasteful—was not the way of history.

Now history had caught up with him and there were two alternatives. He could go out and face the world or he could hide from it. There was no compromise.

Amby picked up the letter between his fingertips, as if it might be something dead and left out in the sun too long. Carefully he dropped it in the wastebasket; then he got his old felt hat and clapped it on his head.

He marched out of the classroom without looking back.

2

When he got home, a scarecrow was perched on the front steps. When it saw him coming, it pulled itself together and got up. "Evening, Doc," it said.

"Good evening, Jake," said Amby.

"I was just fixing to go fishing," Jake told him.

Amby sat down carefully on the steps and shook his head. "Not tonight; don't feel up to it. They're closing down the university."

Jake sat down beside him and stared across the street at the city wilderness. "I suppose that ain't no big surprise to you."

"I've been expecting it," said Amby. "Nobody attends

any more except some *stuffy* kids. All the *nomies* go to
their own universities, if that is what they call them.
Although to tell you the honest truth, Jake, I can't see how
schools like those could give them very much."

"Well, you're fixed all right, I guess," said Jake, con-
solingly. "You been working all these years; you probably
been able to put away a little. Now with me it's different.
We been living hand-to-mouth and we always will."

"I'm not too well fixed," said Amby, "but I'll get along
somehow. I probably haven't too long left; I'm almost
seventy."

"There was a day," said Jake, "when they had a law
that paid a man to quit at sixty five. But the *nomies* threw
that out, just like they did everything."

He picked up a short length of dead branch and dug ab-
sentmindedly at the grass. "I always figured, someday I'd
get me enough together so I could buy a trailer. You can't
do a thing unless you got a trailer. It does beat all how
times can change. I remember when I was a kid it was the
man who owned a house that was all set for life. But now
a house don't count for nothing. You got to have a trailer."

He got up in sections, stood with his rags fluttering in
the wind, looking down at Amby. "You ain't changed your
mind about that fishing, Doc?"

"I'm all beat out," said Amby.

"With you not working any more," Jake said, "us two
can get in a powerful lot of hunting. The place is full of
squirrels and the young rabbits will soon be big enough to
eat. This fall there'll be a sight of coons. Now that you
ain't working, I'll split the skins with you."

"You still can keep the skins," said Amby.

Jake stuck his thumbs into his waistband and spat upon
the ground. "Might just as well spend your time out in
the woods as anywhere. Used to be a man could make
some money if he was lucky at his prowling, but prowling
now is just a waste of time. The places all have been
worked over and it's getting so it's downright dangerous
to go inside of them. You never know when something
might give way and come down and hit you or when the
floor will drop out from underneath you."

He hitched up his britches. "Remember that time we
found the box with all the jewelry in it?"

Amby nodded. "I remember that; you almost got enough to buy the trailer that time."

"Ain't it a fact? It does beat all how a man can fritter cash away. I bought a new gun and a batch of cartridges and some clothes for the family—and God knows, we needed them—and a good supply of grub; and before I knew it there wasn't near enough left over to even think about a trailer. In the old days a man could have bought one on time. All he'd needed would be ten per cent to pay down on it. But you can't do that no more. There ain't even any banks. And no loan companies. Remember, Doc, when the place crawled with loan companies?"

"It all has changed," said Amby. "When I think back it can't seem possible."

But it was, of course.

The city was gone as an institution; the farms had become corporations and people no longer lived in houses— only the *stuffies* and the squatters.

And folks like me, thought Amby.

3

It was a crazy idea—a sign of old age and feeble-mindedness, perhaps. A man of sixty-eight, a man of competence and settled habits, did not go charging off on a wild adventure even if his world had crashed about his ears.

He tried to quit thinking of it, but he couldn't quit. He thought about it all the time that he cooked supper, and while he ate supper, and later when he washed the dishes.

With the dishes done, he went into the living room, carrying the kitchen lamp. He set the lamp on a table beside another lamp and lit the second lamp. *Must be a sign a man's eyes are wearing out,* he thought, *when he needs two lamps to read by.* But kerosene lamps, at best, were poor things; not like electricity.

He picked a book out of the shelves and settled down to read, but he couldn't read; he couldn't keep his mind on what he tried to read. He finally gave it up.

He took one of the lamps, walked to the fireplace and held it high so that the lamplight fell upon the painting there. And he wondered as he raised the lamp if she would smile at him tonight; he was fairly sure she would, for she was always ready with a tiny smile when he needed it the most.

He wasn't sure at first if she were smiling; then he saw she was, and he stood there looking at her and her smile.

There had been many times of late when he talked with her, for he remembered how ready she had always been to listen to him, how he had talked out his troubles and his triumphs—although, come to think of it, his triumphs had been few.

But he could not talk to her tonight; she would not understand. This world in which he lived without her would seem to her so topsy-turvy as to be past all understanding. And if he tried to talk to her about it, she would be disturbed and troubled and he must not let that happen.

You'd think, he told himself, upbraiding himself, that I'd be content to leave well enough alone. I have a place to hide. I could live out my life in comfort and in safety. And that, he knew, was the way he wanted it to be.

But there was that nagging voice which talked inside his brain: *You have failed your task and failed it willingly. You have shut your eyes and failed. You have failed by looking backwards. The true historian does not live in the past alone. He must use the past to understand the present; and he must know them both if he is to see the trend toward the future.*

But I do not want to know the future, said the stubborn Dr. Ambrose Wilson.

And the nagging voice said: *The future is the only thing that is worth the knowing.*

He stood silently, holding the lamp above his head, staring at the painting almost as if he expected it to speak, as if it might give a sign.

There wasn't any sign. There couldn't be a sign, he knew. It was no more than a painting of a woman, dead these thirty years. The sensed nearness, the old sharp memory, the smile upon the lips were in the heart and mind—not in the square of canvas with clever brush strokes that preserved across the years the bright illusion of a loved face.

He lowered the lamp and went back to his chair.

There was so much to say, he thought, and no one to say it to—although the house might listen if he talked to it as an ancient friend. It had been a friend, he thought. It had been lonely often with her no longer here—but not as lonely in the house as away from it, for the house was a part of her.

He was safe here, safe in this anachronistic house, safe in the abandoned city with its empty buildings; comfortable in this city gone back to wilderness, filled with squirrels and rabbits, colorful and fragrant now with the bloom of gone-wild lilacs and escaped daffodils, prowled by squatters who hunted the thickets of its lawns for game and prowled its crumbling structures to find some salvage they might sell.

Queer, he thought, the concepts upon which a culture might be founded, the fantastic acceptance standards which evolved in each society.

Some forty years ago, the cleavage of the culture had first started; it had not come all at once, but quickly enough so that historically it must be regarded as an abrupt rather than a gradual cleavage.

It had been the Year of Crisis, he remembered, when the drums of fear had thudded through the land and a man had lain in bed, tensed and listening for the coming of the bomb, knowing even as he listened that he'd not hear it if it came.

Fear was the start of it, he thought; and what and where would be the end?

He sat huddled in his chair, cringing from the dark barbarism that lay beyond the city—an old man caught between the future and the past.

4

Jake said, "She's a beauty, Doc." He got up to walk around it once again.

"Yes, sir," he said, patting it, "She surely is a beauty. I

don't think I can rightly say I ever saw a finer trailer. And I've seen lots of them."

"We may be doing a lot of traveling in it," Amby told him. "We want one that will stand up. The roads, I understand, aren't what they used to be. The *nomies* chisel on the road tax, and the government hasn't got much money to keep the roads in shape."

"It won't take long," Jake said confidently. "All we got to do is just kind of look around. In no time at all we'll find a camp that will take us in. Stands to reason there'll be one of them that could find a use for us."

He went over to the trailer and carefully wiped a spot of dust off its shiny surface with his ragged shirt sleeve.

"We ain't none of us scarcely slept a wink since you told us, Doc. Myrt, she can't understand it; she keeps saying to me, 'Why is Doc taking us along? We ain't got no claim on him; all we been is neighbors.' "

"I'm a bit too old," said Amby, "to do it by myself. I have to have someone along to help out with the driving and the other chores. And you've been looking forward all these years to going trailering."

"That's a fact," admitted Jake. "Doc, you never spoke a truer word. I wanted it so bad I could almost taste it; and by the looks of it, so have all the rest of us. You ought to see the throwing away and packing that's going on over at the house. Myrt is plain beside herself. I tell you, Doc, it ain't no safe place to go until Myrt calms down a bit."

"Maybe I ought to do some packing myself," said Amby. "Not that there's much to do; I'll just leave the most of it behind."

But he didn't stir. He didn't want to face it.

It would be hard to leave his home—although that was old-fogey thinking, for there were no longer any homes. "Home" was a word out of an era left behind. "Home" was another nostalgic word for old men like him to mumble in their dim remembering. "Home" was the symbol of a static culture that had failed in the scales of Man's survival. To put down roots, to stay and become encumbered by possessions—not only physical, but mental and traditional as well—was to die. To be mobile and forever poised on the edge of flight, to travel lean and gaunt, to shun encumbrances, was the price of freedom and life.

Full cycle, Amby thought—*we have come full cycle. From tribe to city, now back to tribe again.*

Jake came back from the trailer and sat down again. "Tell me, Doc; tell me honest now—why are you doing it? Not that I ain't glad you are, for otherwise I'd never in all my born days get out of this here rat trap. But I can't somehow get it through my head why you are pulling stakes. You ain't a young man, Doc, and . . ."

"I know," said Amby; "maybe that's the reason. Not too much time left, and I have to make the best use of it I can."

"You're sitting pretty, Doc, and not a worry in the world. Now that you've retired, you could take it easy and have a lot of fun."

"I've got to find out," said Amby.

"Find out what?"

"I don't know; just what is happening, I guess."

They sat quietly, looking at the trailer in all its shining glory. From some distance down the street came the faint clatter of pots and pans and a suddenly raised voice.

Myrt still was busy packing.

5

The first evening they stopped at a deserted campsite across the road from an idle factory.

It was an extensive camp and it had the look of being occupied only recently, as if the trailers might have pulled out just a day or two before. There were fresh tire tracks in the dust; scraps of paper still blew about the area, and the ground beneath some of the water faucets still was damp.

Jake and Amby sat in the trailer's shade and looked at the silent buildings just across the road.

"Funny thing," said Jake, "about this place not running. Sign up there says it's a food processing plant. Breakfast food, looks like. Figure maybe it shut down because there wasn't any market for the stuff it makes?"

"That might be it," said Amby. "But seems there should be a market for breakfast cereal, at least some sort of market for it. Enough to keep it running, although maybe not at full capacity."

"Figure there was some kind of trouble?"

"No sign of it," said Amby. "Looks as if they just up and left."

"There's that big house up on the hill. Look, up that-away . . ."

"I see it now," said Amby.

"Might be where the *stuffy* lives."

"Could be."

"Wonder what it would be like to be a *stuffy?* Just sit and watch the cash come rolling in. Let other people work for you. Have everything you want. Never want for nothing."

"I imagine," Amby told him, "that the *stuffies* have their troubles, too."

"I'd like to have them kind of troubles. I'd just plumb love to have them kind of troubles for a year or two."

He spat on the ground and hauled himself erect. "Might go out and see if I could get me a rabbit or a squirrel," he said. "You feel like coming with me?"

Amby shook his head. "I'm a little tuckered out."

"Probably won't find nothing anyhow. Close to a camp like this, the game must be all cleaned out."

"After a while," said Amby, "when I'm rested up a bit, I might take a walk."

6

The house was a *stuffy* house, all right. One could almost smell the money of it. It was large and sprawling, very neatly kept, and surrounded by extensive grounds full of flowers and shrubs.

Amby sat down on a stone wall just outside the grounds and looked back the way he'd come. There below him lay the factory and the deserted camping grounds, with his trailer standing alone in the great level, trampled area. The road wound away to a far horizon, white in the summer sun, and there was nothing on it—not a single car or truck or trailer. And that, he thought, was not the way it had been. Once the roads had been crawling with machines.

But this was a different world than the one he'd known. It was a world that he'd ignored for more than thirty years, and it had grown alien in those thirty years. He had shut himself away from it and lost it; now that he sought it once again, he found it puzzling and at times a little terrifying.

A voice spoke behind him. "Good evening, sir."

Amby turned and saw the man—middle-aged or more, and the tweeds and pipe. Almost, he thought, like the age-old tradition of the English country squire.

"Good evening," Amby said. "I hope I'm not intruding."

"Not at all. I saw you camped down there; very glad to have you."

"My partner went out hunting, so I took a walk."

"You folks changing?"

"Changing?"

"Changing camps, I mean. There used to be a lot of it. Not much any more."

"You mean changing from one camp to another?"

"That's it. A process of settling down, I take it. Get dissatisfied with one setup, so go out and hunt another."

"By now," said Amby, "the shakedown period must be almost over. By now each man must have found his place."

The *stuffy* nodded. "Maybe that's the way it is. I don't know too much about it."

"Nor I," Amby told him. "We're just starting out. My university closed down, so I bought a trailer. My next door neighbors came along with me. This is our first day."

"I've often thought," said the man, "that it might be fun to do a little touring. When I was a boy we used to go on long motoring trips and visit different places; but there doesn't seem to be much of that any more. Used to be places where you could stop the night—motels, they called them. And every mile or so there were eating places and service stations where you could buy gasoline. Now the only place where you can get anything to eat or buy some gas, is at one of the camps; lots of times, I understand, they don't care to sell."

"But we aren't touring. We hope to join a camp."

The *stuffy* stared at him for a moment, then he said: "I wouldn't have thought so, looking at you."

"You don't approve of it?"

"Don't mind me," the *stuffy* said. "Right at this moment, I'm a little sour on them. Just the other morning they all drove out on me. Closed down the plant. Left me sitting here."

He climbed up on the wall and sat down alongside Amby. "They wanted to take me over completely, you understand," he said, settling down to a minute recounting of it. "Under the existing contract they already ran the plant. They bought the raw materials and set up their own work schedules and kept up maintenance. They decided plant operation policy and set production schedules. I'd have had to ask their permission just to go down there and visit. But it wasn't enough for them. Do you know what they wanted?"

Amby shook his head.

"They wanted to take over marketing. That was all that I had left and they wanted to take that away from me. They were all set to shove me out completely. Pay me a percentage of the profit and cut me out entirely."

"Somehow," Amby said, "that doesn't sound quite fair."

"And when I refused to sign, they just packed up and left."

"A strike?"

"I suppose you could call it that. A most effective one."

"What do you do now?"

"Wait until another camp comes down the road. There'll be one along sometime. They'll see the plant standing idle, and if they're industrial and think they can handle it, they'll come up and see me. Maybe we can make a deal. Even if we can't, there'll be another camp along. There's always floating camps. Either that or swarms."

"Swarms?"

"Like bees, you know. A camp gets overcrowded. Too many to handle the contract that they have. So it up and swarms. Usually a bunch of young folks just starting out in life. A swarm is usually easier to deal with than the floaters. The floaters, often as not, are a bunch of radicals and malcontents who can't get along with anyone, while the youngsters in a swarm are anxious to get started at something of their own."

"That all sounds well enough," said Amby, "but how about the ones who left you? Could they afford just to pull stakes and go?"

"They're loaded," said the *stuffy*. "They worked here almost twenty years. They got a sinking fund that would choke a cow."

"I didn't know," said Amby.

There was so much, he thought, that he didn't know. Not only the thinking and the customs, but even a lot of the terminology was strange.

It had been different in the old days when there'd been a daily press; when a new phrase or a new thought became public property almost overnight; when the forces that shaped one's life were daily spread before one in the black and white of print. But now there were no papers and no television. There still was radio, of course; but radio, he thought, was a poor medium to keep a man in touch; even so, it was not the kind of radio he'd known and he never listened to it.

There were no papers and no television, and that wasn't all by any means. There was no furniture, for there was no need of furniture in a trailer with everything built in. There were no rugs, no carpeting, no drapes. There were few luxury items, for there was no room for luxury items in the confines of a trailer. There were no formal and no party clothes, for no one in a trailer camp would dress —there was no room for an extensive wardrobe and the close communal life would discourage all formality. Such dress as there might be in a trailer camp undoubtedly would run heavily to sportswear.

There were no banks or insurance firms or loan companies. Social security had gone down the drain. There was no use for banks or loan companies; the credit union setup, dating from the old trade unionism, would have replaced them on a tight communal basis. And an extension of the old union health and welfare fund, once again on a tight communal basis, had replaced any need of social security, governmental welfare aid, or health insurance. And the war chest idea—once again grafted from unionism—had made each trailer camp an independent, self-sufficient governmental unit.

It worked all right, for there was little that a resident of a trailer camp could spend his money on. The old fly-traps of entertainment; the need of expensive dress; the overhead of house furnishings—all had been wiped out. Thrift had become an enforced virtue—enforced by circumstance.

A man didn't even pay taxes any more—not to speak of, anyhow. State and local governments long ago had fallen by the wayside. There remained nothing but the federal government, and even the federal government had lost much of its control—as it must have known it would on that day of forty years ago. All that need now be paid was a trifling defense tax, and a slightly heavier road tax, and the *nomies* screamed loud and lustily against the paying of the road tax.

"It's not like it used to be," said the *stuffy*. "This trade unionism got entirely out of hand."

"It was about all the people had to tie to," Amby told him. "It was the one surviving piece of logic, the one remaining solid thing that was left to them. Naturally, they embraced it; it took the place of government."

"The government should have done it differently," said the *stuffy*.

"They might have if we hadn't got so frightened. It was the fear that did it; it would have been all right if we hadn't got afraid."

Said the *stuffy:* "We'd been blown plumb to hell if we hadn't got afraid."

"Maybe so," said Amby. "I can remember how it happened. The order went out to decentralize, and I guess industry must have known a good deal more about what the situation was than the most of us; it got out and scattered, without any argument. Maybe they knew the government wasn't fooling and maybe they had some facts that weren't public knowledge. Although the public facts, as I remember them, ran rather to the grim side."

"I was just in my teens then," said the *stuffy*, "but I remember something of it. Real estate worth nothing. Couldn't sell city property at a fraction of its worth. And the workers couldn't stay there, for their jobs had moved away—away out in the country. Decentralization took in a lot of country. The big plants split up, some of them into a lot of smaller units and there had to be a lot of miles between each unit."

Amby nodded. "So there'd be no target big enough for anyone to waste a bomb on. Make it cost too much to wipe out an industry. Where one bomb would have done the job before, now it would take a hundred."

"I don't know," said the *stuffy*, still unwilling to concede. "Seems to me the government could have handled it a little differently instead of letting the thing run on the way it did."

"I suspect the government had a lot on its mind right then."

"Sure it had, but it had been in the housing business up to its ears before. Building all sorts of low-cost housing projects."

"It had the job of helping industry get those new plants set up. And the trailers solved the housing problem for the moment."

"I suppose," the *stuffy* said, "that was the way it was."

And that, of course, was the way it had been.

The workers had been forced to follow their jobs —either follow them or starve. Unable to sell their houses in the cities when the bottom dropped out of the real estate market almost overnight, they compromised on trailers; and around each fractionated industry grew up a trailer camp.

They grew to like the trailer life, perhaps, or they were afraid to build another house for fear the same thing might happen yet again—even if some could afford to build another house, and there were a lot of them who couldn't. Or they may have become disillusioned and disgusted—it did not matter what. But the trailer life had caught on and stayed, and people who were not directly affected by decentralization had gradually drifted into the trailer camps, until even most of the villages stood empty.

The cult of possessions had been forsworn. The tribe sprang up again.

Fear had played its part and freedom—the freedom from possessions, and the freedom to pick up and go without ever looking back—and unionism, too.

For the trailer movement had killed the huge trade union setup. Union bosses and business agents, who had found it easy to control one huge union setup, found it a sheer impossibility to control the hundred scattered units into which each big local had been broken. But within each trailer camp a local brand of unionism had caught on with renewed force and significance. It had served to weld each camp into a solid and cohesive unit. It had made the union a thing close to each family's heart and interest. Unionism, interpreted in the terms of the people and their needs, had provided the tribal pattern needed to make the trailer system work.

"I'll say this much for them," the *stuffy* said. "They were an efficient bunch. They ran the plant better than I could have run it; they watched the costs and they were forever digging up shortcuts and improvements. During the twenty years they worked here they practically redesigned that plant. That's one of the things they pointed out to me in negotiations. But I told them they'd done it to protect their jobs, and that may have been the thing that made them sore enough to leave."

He tapped his pipe out on the wall. "You know," he said, "I'm not too sure but what I'm right. It'll more than likely take any new gang that moves in a month or so to figure out all the jack-leg contraptions that this bunch of mine rigged up. All I hope is that they don't start it up too quick and wreck the whole shebang."

He polished the bowl of his pipe abstractedly. "I don't know. I wish I could figure that tribe out—just for my peace of mind, if nothing else. They were good people and mostly sensible. They were hard workers and up to a month ago easy to get along with. They lived normal lives for the most part, but there were things about them I couldn't understand. Like the superstitions that grew up. They'd worked up a sizeable list of taboos, and they were hell on signs of exorcism and placation. Oh, sure, I know we used to do it—cross your fingers and spit over your left shoulder and all that sort of stuff—but with us it was all in fun. It was just horseplay with us. A sort of loving link with a past we were reluctant to give up. But these people, I swear, believed and lived by it."

"That," said Amby, "bears out my own belief that the

culture has actually degenerated into the equivalent of tribalism, perhaps further than I thought. Your small, compact, enclosed social groups give rise to that sort of thing. In a more integrated culture, such notions are laughed out of existence; but in protected soil they take root and grow."

"The farm camps are the worst," the *stuffy* told him. "They have rainmaking mumbo-jumbo and crop magic and all the rest of it."   ·

Amby nodded. "That makes sense. There's something about the enigma of the soil and seed that encourages mysticism. Remember the wealth of mythology that grew up around agriculture in prehistorical times—the fertility rites, and the lunar planting tables, and all the other fetishes."

He sat on the stone wall, staring off across the land; out of the dark unknown of the beginning of the race, he seemed to hear the stamp of calloused feet, the ritual chant, the scream of the sacrifice.

7

The next day, from the top of a high hill, they sighted the farm camp. It was located at the edge of a grove of trees a little distance from a row of elevators, and across the plains that stretched in all directions lay the goldgreen fields.

"Now that's the kind of place I'd like to settle into," said Jake. "Good place to raise the kids and it stands to reason you wouldn't have to kill yourself with work. They do farming mostly with machinery and you'd just ride around, steering a tractor or a combine or a baler or something of the sort. Good healthful living, too, out in the sun and open air and you'd get to see some country, more than likely. When the harvest is done the whole kit and caboodle would just pull stakes and go somewhere else. Out to the southwest maybe for the lettuce or the other garden stuff, or out to the coast for fruit or maybe even south. I don't know if there's any winter farming in the south. Maybe you know, Doc."

"No, I don't," said Amby.

He sat beside Jake and watched Jake drive; Jake, he admitted to himself, was a fine man at the wheel; a man felt safe and confident with Jake driving. He never went too fast; he took no chances, and he knew how to treat a car.

In the back seat the kids were raising a ruckus, and now Jake turned his attention to them. "If you young'uns don't quiet down, I'm going to stop this here outfit and give you all a hiding. You kids know right well you wouldn't be raising all this rumpus if your Ma was with you instead of back there in the trailer. She'd smack your ears for fair and she'd get you quietened down."

The kids paid no attenion, went on with their scuffling.

"I been thinking," Jake said to Amby, his duty as a father now discharged, "that maybe this is the smartest thing you ever done. Maybe you should have done it sooner. Stands to reason an educated man like you won't have no trouble finding a good place in one of these here camps. Ain't likely they got many educated men and there's nothing, I've always said, like an education. Never got one myself and maybe that's why I set such a store by it. One of the things I hated back there in the city was watching them kids run wild without a lick of learning. Myrt and me did the best we could, but neither of us know much more than our ABC's and we weren't proper teachers."

"They probably have schools in all the camps," said Amby. "I've never heard they had, but they have some sort of universities—and before anyone could go to college he'd have to have some sort of elementary education. I rather imagine we'll find the camps equipped with a fair communal program. A camp is a sort of mobile village and more than likely it would be run like one, with schools and hospitals and churches and all the other things you'd expect to find in towns—although all of them, I imagine, will have certain overtones of trade unionism. Culture is a strange thing, Jake, but it usually spells out to pretty much the same in the end result. Differing cultures are no more than different approaches to a common problem."

"I declare," said Jake, "it's a pleasure just to sit here

and listen to all that lingo that you throw around. And the beauty of it is you sound just like you know what all them big words mean."

He swung the car off the highway onto the rutted road that ran up to the camp. He slowed to a crawl and they bumped along.

"Look at it," he said. "Ain't it a pretty sight. See all that washing hung out on the lines and those posies growing in the window boxes on the trailers and that little picket fence some of the folks have set up around the trailers, just like the yards back home. I wouldn't be none surprised, Doc, if we find these folks people just like us."

They reached the camp and swung out of the road, off to one side of the trailers. A crowd of children had gathered and stood watching them. A woman came to the door of one of the trailers and stood, leaning against the doorway, staring at them. Some dogs joined the children and sat down to scratch fleas.

Jake got out of the car. "Hello, kids," he said.

They giggled shyly at him.

Jake's kids piled out of the back seat and stood in a knot beside their father.

Myrt climbed down out of the trailer. She fanned herself with a piece of cardboard. "Well, I never," she declared.

They waited.

Finally an old man came around the end of one of the trailers and walked toward them. The kids parted their ranks to let him through. He walked slowly, with a cane to help him. "Something I can do for you, stranger?"

"We was just looking around," said Jake.

"Look all you want," the oldster told him.

He glanced at Amby, still sitting in the car. "Howdy, oldtimer."

"Howdy," said Amby.

"Looking for anything special, oldtimer?"

"I guess you could say we are looking for a job; we hope to find a camp that will take us on."

The old man shook his head. "We're pretty well full up. But you better talk to the business agent; he's the one to see."

He turned and yelled to the group of staring kids. "You kids go and hunt up Fred."

They scattered like frightened partridges.

"We don't get many folks like you any more," the old man said. "Years ago there were lots of them, just drifting along, looking for whatever they could find. A lot of folks from the smaller towns and a lot of them DF's."

He saw the look of question on Amby's face.

"Displaced farmers," he said. "Ones who couldn't make a go of it and once they took off parity there were a lot of them. Maddest bunch you ever saw. Fighting mad, they were. Had come to count on parity; thought they had it coming to them. Figured the government had done them dirt and I suppose it had. But it did dirt to a lot of the rest of us as well. You couldn't bust things up the way they were busted up without someone getting hurt. And the way things were, you coudn't expect the government to keep on with all their programs. Had to simplify."

Amby nodded in agreement. "You couldn't maintain a top-heavy bureaucracy in a system that had become a technological tribal system."

"I guess you're right," the old man agreed in turn. "So far as the farmers were concerned, it didn't make much difference anyhow. The small land holdings were bound to disappear. The little farmer just couldn't make the grade. Agriculture was on its way toward corporate holdings even before D. C. Machinery was the thing that did it. You couldn't farm without machinery and it didn't pay to buy machinery to handle the few acres on the smaller farms."

He walked closer to the car and stroked one fender with a gnarled hand. "Good car you got here."

"Had it for a long time," Amby told him. "Took good care of it."

The old man brightened. "That's a rule we got around here, too. Everyone has to take good care of everything. Ain't like it was one time when, if you busted something, or it wore out, or you lost it, you could run down the corner and get another one. Pretty good camp that way. Young fellers spend a lot of their spare time dinging up the cars. You should see what they've done to some of them. Yes, sir, there's some of them cars they've made almost human."

He walked up to the open car window and leaned on the door. "Darn good camp," he said. "Anyway you look at it. We got the neatest crops around; and we take good good care of the soil; and that's worth a lot to the *stuffy* who owns the place. We been coming back to this same place every spring for almost twenty years. If someone beats us here, the *stuffy* won't even talk to them. He always waits for us. There ain't many camps, I can tell you, that can say as much. Of course, in the winter we wander around considerable but that's because we want to. There ain't a winter place we been we couldn't go back to anytime we wanted."

He eyed Amby speculatively. "You wouldn't know nothing about rain-making, now would you?"

"Some years ago I did some reading on what had been done about it," Amby told him. "Cloud seeding, they called it. But I forget what they used. Silver—something. Some kind of chemical."

"I don't know anything about this seeding," the old man said; "and I don't know if they use chemicals or not."

"Of course," he said, anxious not to be misunderstood, "we got a bunch of the finest rain-makers that you ever saw, but in this farming business you can't have too many of them. Better to have one or two too many than one or two too few."

He looked up at the sky. "We don't need no rain right now and it ain't right to use the power, of course, unless you have some need of it. I wish you'd come when we needed rain, for then you could stay over and see the boys in action. They put on quite a show. When they put on a dance everyone turns out to watch."

"I read somewhere once," said Amby, "about the Navahos. Or maybe it was the Hopis . . ."

But the old man wasn't interested in Navahos or Hopis. "We got a fine crew of green-thumbers, too," he said. "I don't want to sound like bragging, but we got the finest crew . . ."

The children came charging around the parked trailers, yelling. The old man swung around. "Here comes Fred."

Fred ambled toward them. He was a big man, bareheaded, with an unruly thatch of black hair, bushy eyebrows, a mouthful of white teeth. "Hello, folks," he said. "What can I do for you?"

Jake explained.

Fred scratched his head, embarrassed and perplexed. "We're full up right now; fact is, we're just on the edge of swarming. I don't see how we can take on another family. Not unless you could offer something special."

"I'm handy at machinery," Jake told him; "I can drive anything."

"We got a lot of drivers. How about repair? Know anything about welding? Can you operate a lathe?"

"Well, no . . ."

"We have to repair our own machines and keep them in top running shape. Sometimes we have to make parts to replace ones that have been broken. Just can't wait to get replacements from the factory, we're kind of jacks-of-all-trades around here. There's a lot more to it than driving. Anyone can drive. Even the women and the kids."

"Doc here," said Jake, "is an educated man. Was a professor at the university until the university shut down. Maybe you could find some use . . ."

Fred cheered up. "You don't say. Not agronomy . . ."

"History," Amby told him, "I don't know anything but history."

"Now that's too bad," said Fred. "We could use an agronomist. We're trying to run some experimental plots, but we don't know too much about it. We don't seem to get nowhere."

The old man said to Amby: "The idea is to develop better strains. It's our stock in trade. One of our bargaining points. Each camp furnishes its own seed and you can get a better deal out of the *stuffy* if you have top-notch strains. We got a good durham, but we're working on corn now. If we could get some that matured ten days sooner, say . . ."

"It sounds interesting," said Amby, "but I couldn't help you. I don't know a thing about it."

"I'd sure work hard," said Jake, "if you just gave me a chance. You wouldn't find a more willing worker in your entire camp."

"Sorry," the business agent told him. "We all are willing workers. If you're looking for a place your best bet would be a swarm. They might take you in. An old camp like us don't take newcomers as a rule; not unless they got something special."

"Well," said Jake, "I guess that's it."

He opened the door and got into the car. The kids swarmed into the back seat. Myrt climbed back into the trailer.

"Thanks," Jake said to the business agent. "Sorry we took up your time."

He swung the car around and bumped back to the road. He was silent for a long time. Finally he spoke up. "What the hell," he asked, "is an agronomist?"

8

That was the way it was everywhere they went:

—*Are you one of these cybernetic fellows? No? Too bad. We sure could use one of those cybernetic jerks.*

—*Too bad. We could use a chemist. Messing around with fuels. Don't know a thing except what we dig out. One of these days the boys will blow the whole camp plumb to hell.*

—*Now if you were a lifter. We could use a lifter.*

—*You know electronics, maybe. No? Too bad.*

—*History. Afraid we got no use for history.*

—*You know any medicine? Our Doc is getting old.*

—*Rocket engineer? We got some ideas. We need a guy like that.*

—*History? Nope. What would we do with history?*

But there was a use for history, Amby told himself. "I know there is a use for it," he said. "It has always been a tool before. Now, suddenly, even in a raw, new society such as this, it could not have lost its purpose."

He lay in his sleeping bag and stared up at the sky.

Back home, he thought, it was already autumn; the leaves were turning and the city, in the blaze of autumn, he recalled, was a place of breathless beauty.

But here, deep in the south, it still was summer and

there was a queer, lethargic feel to the deep green of the foliage and the flinthard blueness of the sky—as if the green and blue were stamped upon the land and would remain forever, a land where change had been outlawed and the matrix of existence had been hardcast beyond any chance of alteration.

The trailer loomed black against the sky; now that Jake and Myrt had quit their mumbling talk inside of it, he could hear the purling of the stream that lay just beyond the campsite. The campfire had died down until it was no more than a hint of rose in the whiteness of the ash, and from the edge of the woods a bird struck up a song— a mocking bird, he thought, although not so sweet a song as he had imagined a mocking bird would sing.

That was the way it was with everything, he thought. Nothing was the way you imagined it. Most often a thing would be less glamorous and more prosaic than one had imagined it; and then, suddenly, in some unexpected place one would encounter something that would root him in his tracks.

The camps, once he'd seen two or three of them, had fallen into pattern—good solid American, sound business-practice patterns; the peculiarities had ceased to be peculiarities once he had come to understand the reason for them.

Like the weekly military drills, for instance, and the regular war games, with every man-Jack of the camp going through maneuvers or working out in all seriousness, grimly, without any horseplay, a military problem—with the women and the children scattering like coveys of quail to seek out hiding places from imaginary foes.

And that was why, he knew, the federal government could get along on its trifling defense tax. For here, at hand, subject to instantaneous call, was a citizen soldiery that would fight a total, terrible war such as would rip to pieces and hunt down with frontier efficiency and Indian savagery any enemy that might land upon the continent. The federal government maintained the air force, supplied the weapons, conducted the military research and provided the overall command and planning. The people, down to the last and least of them, were the standing army, ready for instant mobilization, trained to hair-trigger readiness, and operative without a dime of federal cost.

It was a setup, he realized now, having seen the war games and the drill, that would give pause to any potential enemy. It was something new in the science of warfare. Here stood a nation that presented no target worth the bomb that might be dropped upon it, fostering no cities to be seized and held, no industries which might be ravaged in their entirety, and with every male inhabitant between the ages of 16 and 70 a ready, willing fighter.

He lay there, pondering the many things he'd seen, the strangely familiar and the unfamiliar.

Like the folkways that had grown up within each camp, compounded of legend, superstition, magic, remembered teachings, minor hero-worship and all the other inevitable odds and ends of close communal living. And the folkways, he realized, were a part of the fierce, partisan loyalty of each man and woman for their own home camp. Out of this had arisen the fantastic rivalry, hard at times to understand, which existed among the camps, manifesting itself all the way from the bragging of the small fry to the stiff-necked refusal of camp leaders to share their knowledge or their secrets with any other camp. Hard to understand, all of it, until one saw in it the translation of the old tradition that had been the soul and body of American business practice.

A queer layout, thought Dr. Ambrose Wilson, lying in his sleeping bag in the depth of southern night—a queer layout, but a most effective one, and understandable within its terms of reference.

Understandable except for one thing—something on which he could not lay a finger. A feeling, perhaps, rather than a fact—a feeling that somewhere, somehow, underneath this whole new fabric of the neo-gypsy life, lay some new factor, vital and important, that one could sense but could never lay a name to.

He lay there, thinking of that new and vital factor, trying to sift out and winnow the impressions and the clues. But there was nothing tangible; nothing to reach out and grasp; nothing that one could identify. It was like chaff without a single grain, like smoke without a fire—it was something new and, like all the other things, perhaps, entirely understandable within its frame of reference. But where was the reference, he wondered.

They had come down across the land, following the great river, running north to south, and they'd found many camps—crop camps with great acreages of grain and miles of growing corn; industrial camps with smoking chimneys and the clanking of machines; transportation camps with the pools of trucks and the fantastic operation of a vast freightage web; dairy camps with herds of cattle and the creameries and cheese factories where the milk was processed and the droves of hogs that were a sideline to the dairying; chicken camps; truck farming camps; mining camps; road maintenance camps; lumbering camps and all the others. And now and then the floaters and the swarms, wanderers like themselves, looking for a place.

Everywhere they'd gone it had been the same. A chorus of "too bad" resounding down the land, the swarms of staring children and the scratching dogs and the business agent saying there was nothing.

Some camps had been friendlier than others; in some of these they'd stayed for a day or week to rest up from their travels, to overhaul the motor, to get the kinks out of their legs, to do some visiting.

In those camps he had walked about and talked, sitting in the sun or shade, as the time of day demanded; it had seemed at times he had got to know the people. But always, when it seemed that he had got to know them, he'd sense the subtle strangeness, the nebulous otherness, as if there were someone he could not see sitting in the circle, someone staring at him from some hidden spying spot, and he'd know then that there lay between him and these people a finely-spun fabric of forty years forgotten.

He listened to their radios, communal versions of the 1960 ham outfits, and heard the ghostly voices come in from other camps, some nearby, some a continent away, a network of weird communication on the village level. Gossip, mostly, but not entirely gossip, for some of it was official messages—the placing of an order for a ton of cheese or a truckload of hay, or the replacement for some broken machine part—or possibly the confirmation of a debt that one camp owed another for some merchandise or product, and oftentimes a strange shuffling of those debts from one camp to another, promise paying promise. And what of it was gossip had a special sense, imprinted with the almost unbelievable pattern of this fantastic culture which over night had walked out of its suburbia to embrace nomadism.

And always there was magic, a strangely gentle magic used for the good of people rather than their hurt. It was, he thought, as if the brownies and the fairies had come back again after their brief banishment from a materialistic world. There were quaint new ceremonies drawing from the quaintness of the old; there were good-luck charms and certain words to say; there was a resurgence of old and simple faith forgotten in the most recent of our yesterdays, an old and simple faith in certain childish things. *And, perhaps,* he thought, *it is well that it is so.*

But the most puzzling of all was the blending of the ancient magic and the old beliefs with an interest just as vital in modern technology—cybernetics going hand in hand with the good luck charm, the rain dance and agronomy crouching side by side.

All of it bothered him in more ways than one as he sought an understanding of it, tried to break down the pattern and graph it mentally on a historic chart sheet; for as often as the graph seemed to work out to some sensible system it would be knocked out of kilter by the realization he was working with no more than surface evidence.

There was always something missing—that sensed and vital factor.

They had traveled down the continent to a chorus of "too bad"; Jake, he knew, was a worried man, as he had every right to be. Lying in his sleeping bag night after night, he'd listened to them talking—Jake and Myrt— when the kids had been asleep and he should have been. And while he'd taken care, out of decency, not to be close enough or listen hard enough to catch their actual words, he had gathered from the tones of their mumbling voices what they had talked about.

It was a shame, he thought; Jake's hopes had been so high and his confidence so great. It was a terrible thing, he told himself, to see a man lose his confidence, a little day by day—to see it drain away from him like blood-drip from a wound.

He stirred, settling his body ino the sleeping bag, and shut his eyes against the stars. He felt sleep advance upon him like an ancient comforter; and in that hazy moment he had drifted from the world and yet not entirely lost it, he saw once again, idealized and beautiful, the painting that hung above the fireplace, with the lamplight falling on it.

9

The trailer was gone when he awoke.

He did not realize it at first, for he lay warm and comfortable, with the fresh wind of morning at his face, listening to the gladness of the birds from each tree and thicket, and the talking of the brook as it flowed among its pebbles.

He lay thinking how fine it was to be alive and vaguely wondering what the day would bring and thankful that he did not fear to meet it.

It was not until then that he saw the trailer was no longer there; he lay quietly for a moment, uncomprehending, before the force of what had happened slapped him in the face.

The first wave of panic washed over him and swiftly ebbed away—the cold fear of loneness, the panic of desertion—retreating before the dull red glow of anger. He found his clothes inside the sleeping bag and swiftly scrambled out. Sitting on the bag to dress, he took in the scene and tried to reconstruct how it might have happened.

The camp lay just beyond a long dip in the road and he remembered how they had blocked the trailer's wheels against the slope of ground. More than likely Jake had simply taken away the blocks, released the brakes, and rolled down the hill, not starting the motor until well out of hearing.

He got up from the sleeping bag and walked numbly forward. Here were the stones they'd used to block the trailer and there the tracks of the tires straight across the dew.

And something else: Leaning against a tree was the .22 rifle that had been Jake's most prized possession and beside it an old and bulging haversack.

He knelt beside the tree and unstrapped the haversack. There were two cartons of matches, ten boxes of ammunition, his extra clothing, food, cooking and eating utensils, and an old raincoat.

He knelt there, looking at it all spread upon the ground and he felt the burning of the tears just behind his eyelids. Treachery, sure—but not entirely treacherous, for they'd not forgotten him. Thievery and desertion and the worst of bad intentions, yet Jake had left him the rifle that had been his good right arm.

Those mumbled conversations that he had listened to— could they have been plotting rather than just worried talk? And what if he had listened to the words rather than the mumble, what if he had crept and listened and learned what they were planning—what could he have done about it?

He repacked the haversack and carried it and the rifle to his sleeping bag. It would be a lot to carry, but he would take it slow and easy and he would get along. As a matter of fact, he consoled himself, he was not too badly off; he still had his billfold and the money that remained. He wondered, without caring much, how Jake, without a cent, would get gasoline and food when he needed it.

And he could hear Jake saying, in those mumbled nightly talks: *"It's Doc. That's why they won't take us in. They take one look at him and know the day is not far off when he'll be a welfare charge. They aren't taking on someone who'll be a burden to them in a year or two."*

Or: *"It's Doc, I tell you, Myrt. He flings them big words around and they are scared of him. Figure he won't fit. Figure he is snooty. Now take us. We're common, ordinary folks. They'd take us like a shot if we weren't packing Doc."*

Or: *"Now us, we can do any kind of work, but Doc is specialized. We won't get nothing unless we cut loose from Doc."*

Amby shook his head. It was funny, he thought, to

what lengths a man would go once he got desperate enough. Gratitude and honor, even friendship, were frail barriers to the actions of despair.

And I, he asked himself. What do I do now?

Certainly not the first thing that had popped into his head—turning around and heading back for home. That would be impossible; in another month or so, snow would have fallen in the north and he would be unable to get through. If he decided to go home, he'd have to wait till spring.

There was one thing to do—continue southward, traveling as he had been traveling, but at a slower pace. There might even be some merit in it. He would be by himself and would have more time to think. And here was a situation that called for a lot of thinking, a lot of puzzling out. Somewhere, he knew, there had to be an answer and a key to that factor he had sensed within the camps. Once he had that factor, the history graph could be worked out, and he would have done the task he had set out to do.

He left the haversack and rifle on the sleeping bag and walked out to the road. He stood in the middle of it, looking first one way and then the other. It was a long and lonely road and he must travel it as lonely as the road. He'd never had a child, and of recent years he'd scarcely had a friend. Jake, he admitted now, had been his closest friend; but Jake was gone, cut off from him not only by the distance and the winding road, but by this act which now lay between them.

He squared his shoulders, with an outward show of competence and bravery which he did not feel, and walked back to pick up the sleeping bag, the haversack and rifle.

10

It was a month later that he stumbled on the truckers camp, quite by accident.

It was coming on toward evening; he was on the lookout for a place to spend the night when he approached the intersection and saw the semi-trailer parked there.

A man was squatted beside a newly-lighted campfire,

carefully feeding small sticks to the flame. A second man was unpacking what appeared to be a grub-box. A third was coming out of the woods with a bucket, probably carrying water from a nearby stream.

The man tending the fire saw Amby, and stood up. "Howdy, stranger," he called. "Looking for a place to camp?"

Amby nodded and approached the campfire. He took the haversack and sleeping bag off his shoulder and dropped them to the ground. "I'd be much obliged."

"Glad to have you," said the man. He hunkered down beside the fire again and went on nursing it. "Ordinarily we don't camp out for the night. We just stop long enough to cook a bite to eat, then hit the road again. We got a bunk in the job so one of us can sleep while another drives. Even Tom has got so he's pretty good at driving."

He nodded at the man who had brought in the water. "Tom ain't a trucker. He's a perfesser at a university, on a leave of absence."

Tom grinned across the fire at Amby. "Sabbatical."

"So am I," said Amby. "Mine is permanent."

"But tonight we'll make a night of it," went on the trucker. "I don't like the sound of the motor. She's heating up some, too. We'll have to tear it down."

"Tear it down right here?"

"Why not? Good a place as any."

"But . . ."

The trucker chuckled. "We'll get along all right. Jim, my helper over there—he's a lifter. He'll just h'ist her out and bring her over to the fire and we'll tear her down."

Amby sat down by the fire. "I'm Amby Wilson," he said. "Just wandering around."

"Rambling far?"

"From up in Minnesota."

"Far piece of walking for a man your age."

"I came part of the way by car."

"Car break down on you?"

"My partner ran off with it."

"Now," the trucker said, judiciously, "that's what I'd call a lousy, lowdown trick."

"Jake didn't mean any harm; he just got panicky."

"You try to track him down?"

"What's the use of trying? There's no way that I can."

"You could get a tracer."

"What's a tracer?"

"Pop," the trucker asked, "where the hell you been?"

And it was a fair question, Amby admitted to himself.

"A tracer," said Tom, "is a telepath. A special kind of telepath. He can track down a mind and find it almost every time. A kind of human bloodhound. It's hard work and there aren't many of them; but as the years go by we hope there will be more—and better."

A tracer is a telepath!

Just like that, without any warning.

A special kind of telepath—as if there might be many other kinds of them.

Amby sat hunched before the fire and looked cautiously around to catch the sheltered grin. But they were not grinning; they acted, he thought, as if this matter of a telepath was very commonplace.

Could it be that here, he wondered, within minutes after meeting them, these people had been the first to say the word that made some sense out of the welter of folklore and magic he'd encountered in the camps?

A tracer was a telepath; and a lifter might be a teleporter; and a green-thumber very well might be someone who had an inherent, exaggerated sympathy and understanding for the world of living things.

Was this, then, the missing factor he had sought; the differentness sensed in the camps; the logic behind the rainmakers and all the other mumbo-jumbo that he had thought of as merely incidental to an enclosed social group?

He brought his hands together between his knees, locking his fingers together tightly, to keep from trembling. *Good Lord*, he thought, *if this is it, so many things explained! If this is the answer that I sought, then here is a culture that is unbeatable!*

Tom broke in upon his thinking. "You said you were on a sabbatical as well as I. A permanent one, you said. Are you a school man, too?"

"I was," said Amby, "but the university closed down. It was one of the old universities, and there was no money and not many students."

"You're looking for another school post?"

"I'd take anything; it seems that no one wants me."

"The schools are short on men. They would snap you up."

"You mean these trailer universities."

Tom nodded. "That is what I mean."

"You don't think much of them?" the trucker asked, his hackles rising.

"I don't know anything about them."

"They're good as any schools there ever were," the trucker said. "Don't let no one tell you different."

Amby hunched forward toward the fire, the many questions, the hope and fear bubbling in his mind. "This tracer business," he said. "You said a tracer was a special kind of telepath. Are there others—I mean, are there other possibilities?"

"Some," said Tom. "There seems to be a lot of special talent showing up these days. We catch a lot of them in the universities and we try to train them, but there isn't much that we can do. After all, how could you or I train a telepath? How would you go about it? About the best that we can do is to encourage each one of them to use such talent as he has to the best advantage."

Amby shook his head, confused. "But I don't understand. Why do you have them now when we never used to have them?"

"Perhaps there may have been some of them before D. C. There must have been, for the abilities must have been there, latent, waiting for their chance. But maybe, before this, they never had a chance. Maybe they were—well, killed in the rush. Or the abilities that there were may have been smothered under the leveling influence of the educational system. There may have been some who had the talents, and were afraid to use them for fear of being different in a culture where differentness was something to point a finger at. And being afraid, they suppressed them, until they weren't bothered by them. And there may have been others who used their talents secretly to their own advantage. Can you imagine what a lawyer or a politician or a salesman could have done with telepathy?"

"You believe this?"

"Well, not all of it. But the possibilities exist."

"What do you believe, then?"

"Folks are smarter now," the trucker said.

"No, Ray, that isn't it at all. The people are the same. Perhaps there were special talents back before D. C., but I don't think they showed up as often as they show up now. We got rid of a lot of the old restrictions and conventionalities. We threw away a lot of the competition and the pressure when we left the houses, and all the other things we had thought we couldn't get along without. We cut out the complexities. Now no one is breathing down our necks. We don't have to worry so much about keeping up with the man next door—because the man next door has become a friend and is no longer a yardstick of our social and economic station. We aren't trying to pack forty-eight hours of living into every twenty-four. Maybe we're giving ourselves the chance to develop what we missed before."

Jim, the helper, had hung a pot of coffee on a forged stick over the fire and now was cutting meat.

"Pork chops tonight," said Ray, the trucker. "We were passing by a farm camp this morning and there was this pig out in the road and there wasn't nothing I could do . . ."

"You almost wrecked the truck to get him."

"Now, that's a downright libel," Ray protested. "I did my level best to miss him."

Jim went on cutting chops, throwing them into a big frying pan as he sliced them off.

"If you're looking for a teaching job," said Tom, "all you got to do is go to one of the universities. There are a lot of them. Most of them not large."

"But where do I find them?"

"You'd have to ask around. They moved around a lot. Get tired of one place and go off to another. But you're lucky now. The south is full of them. Go north in the spring, come south in the fall."

The trucker had settled back on his haunches and was building himself a cigaret. He lifted the paper to his mouth and licked it, twirling it in shape. He stuck it in his mouth and it drooped there limply while he hunted for a small twig from the fire to give himself a light.

"Tell you what," he said, "why don't you just come along with us? There's room for everyone. Bound to find a bunch of universities along the way. You can have your pick of them. Or you might take it in your mind to stick with us right out to the coast. Tom is going out there to see some shirt-tail relatives of his."

Tom nodded. "Sure. Why don't you come along."

"Ain't like it was in the old days," said the trucker. "My old man was a trucker then. You went hell-for-leather. You didn't stop for nothing—not even to be human. You just kept rolling."

"That was the way with all of us," said Amby.

"Now we take it easy," said the trucker. "We don't get there as fast, but we have a lot more fun and there ain't no one suffering if we're late a day or two."

Jim put the pan of chops on the bed of coals.

"It's a lot easier trucking, too," said Ray, "if you can get a lifter for a helper. Nothing to loading or unloading if you have a lifter. And if you get stuck in the mud, he can push you out. Jim here is the best lifter that I ever saw. He can lift that big job if he has to without any trouble. But you got to keep after him; he's the laziest mortal I ever saw."

Jim went on frying chops.

The trucker flipped the cigaret toward the fire and it landed in the pan of chops. Almost immediately it rose out of them; described a tiny arc and fell into the coals.

Jim said: "Ray, you got to cut out things like that. Watch what you are doing. You wear me out just picking up behind you."

The trucker said to Amby, "How about joining up with us? You'd see a lot of country."

Amby shook his head. "I'll have to think about it."

But he was dissembling. He didn't have to think about it.

He knew he wasn't going.

II

He stood by the dead campfire at the intersection and

waved goodbye to them, watching the semi-trailer disappear down the road in the early morning mist.

Then he bent down and picked up the haversack and the sleeping bag and slung them on his shoulder.

He felt within himself a strange urgency—a happy urgency. And it was fine to feel it once again after all these months. Fine again to know he had a job to do.

He stood for a moment, staring around at the camping grounds—the dead ash of the fire, the pile of unused wood, and the great spot on the ground where the grease from the motor of the truck soaked slowly in the soil.

He would not have believed it, he knew, if he had not seen it done—seen Jim lift the motor from the truck once the bed bolts had been loosened, lift it and guide it to rest beside the fire without once laying hands upon it. Again he had watched the stubborn nuts that defied the wrench turn slowly and reluctantly without a tool upon them, then spin freely to rise free of the thread and deposit themselves neatly in a row.

Once, long ago it seemed, he'd talked with a *stuffy* who had told him how efficiently a camp had run his plant, complaining all the while of how they'd rejiggered it until it would take any other camp a month at least to figure out the sheer mechanics of it.

Efficient! Good Lord, of course they were efficient! What new methods, what half-guessed new principles, he wondered, may have gone into that rejiggered plant?

All over the country, he wondered, how many new principles and methods might there be at work? But not regarded as new principles by the camps that had worked them out; regarded rather as trade secrets, as powerful points in bargaining, as tribal stock-in-trade. And in the whole country, he wondered, how many new talents might there be, how many applicable variations of those specific talents?

A new culture, he thought—an unbeatable culture if it only knew its strength, if it could be jarred out of its provincialism, if it could strip from its new abilities the veil of superstition. And that last, he knew, might be the toughest job of all; the magic had been used to cloak annoying ignorance and as an explanation for misunderstanding. It offered a simple and an easy explanation, and it might be hard to substitute in its stead the realization that at the moment there could be little actual knowledge and no complete understanding—only an acceptance and a patience against the day when it might be understood.

He walked over to the tree where he had leaned his rifle and picked it up. He swung it almost gayly in his hand and was astonished at the familiarity of it, almost as if it were a part of him, an extension of his hand.

And that was the way it was with these people and the possibilities. They'd gotten so accustomed to the magic, that it had become a part of everyday; they did not see the greatness of it.

The possibilities, once one thought of them, were fantastic. Develop the abilities and within another hundred years the sputtering radios would be gone, replaced by telepaths who would blanket the nation with a flexible network of communications that never would break down, that would be immune to atmospheric conditions—an intelligent, human system of communication without the inherent limitations of an electronic setup.

The trucks would be gone, too, with relays of teleporters whisking shipments from coast to coast (and all points in between), fast and smooth and without a hitch and, once again, without regard to weather or to road conditions.

And that was only two facets of the picture. What of all the others—the known, the suspected, the now-impossible?

He walked from the campsite out to the road and stood for a moment, wondering. Where was that camp where they had asked if he was a rocket engineer? And where had been the camp that had been in the market for a chemist because the boys were fooling around with fuels? And where, he wondered, would he be able to pick up a lifter? And perhaps a good, all-purpose telepath.

It wasn't much, this thing he had in mind, he admitted to himself. But it was a start. "Give me ten years," he said. "Just ten years is all I ask."

But even if he had no more than two, he had to make a start. For if he made the start, then perhaps there'd be someone who would carry on. Someone had to make a start. Someone like himself, perhaps, who could look upon this neo-tribal world objectively and in the light of the historic past. *And there may not be many of us left,* he thought.

He might have a hard job selling them, he knew, but he thought he knew the pitch.

He set off up the road and he whistled as he went.

It wasn't much, but it would be spectacular if he could accomplish it. Once it had been done, it would be a thing that every camp would spy and scheme and cheat and steal to do.

And it would take something such as that, he knew, to knock some sense into their heads; to make them see the possibilities; to set them to wondering how they might turn to use the other strange abilities which had blossomed here in the soil of a new society.

Now where was that camp where they'd been in need of a rocket engineer?

Up the road somewhere. Up the winding, lonely road that was no longer lonely.

Just up the road a piece. A hundred miles or two. Or was it more than that?

He jogged along, trying to remember. But it was hard to remember. There had been so many days and so many camps. A landmark, he thought—I was always good at landmarks.

But there had been too many landmarks, too.

12

He wandered up the road, stopping at the camps and the answer that he got became monotonous.

"Rockets? Hell, no! Who'd fool around with rockets?"

And he wondered: Had there ever been a camp where they'd said they could use a rocket engineer? Who would fool around with rockets? What would be the use of it?

The word went ahead of him, by telepath perhaps, by radio, by fast-running word of mouth, and he found himself a legend. He found them waiting for him, as if they had been expecting him, and they had a standard greeting that soon became a joke.

"You the gent who's looking for the rockets?"

But with their joking and the legend of him, he became one of them; and yet, even in becoming one of them, he still stood apart from them and saw the greatness that they missed, a greatness that they had to—*had to*—be awakened to. And a greatness that mere words and preaching would never make come alive for them.

He sat at the nightly communal gabfests, slept in those trailers that had room for an extra person, and helped at little tasks and listened to the yarning. And in turn did some yarning of his own. Time after time he felt again the strangeness and the otherness; but now that he recognized it, it did not disturb him—and sometimes, looking around the circle, he could spot the one who had it.

Lying in a bunk at night, before he went to sleep, he thought a lot about it and finally it all made sense to him.

These abilities had been with Man always, perhaps even from the caves, but then, as now, Man had not understood the power and so had not followed it. Rather he had followed along another path—ignoring mind for hand—and had built himself a wonderful and impressive and complex culture of machines. He'd built with his hands and with mighty labor the vast, complex machines which did what he might have done with the power of mind alone had he but chosen to do so. Rather he had hidden the mental power behind semantics of his own devising, and in seeking after intellectual status had laughed into disrepute the very thing he sought.

This thing which had happened, Amby told himself, was no quirk in the development of the race, but as sure and certain as the sun. It was no more than a returning to the path it had been intended all along that Man should follow. After centuries of stumbling, the human race once more was headed right again. And even if there had been no decentralization, no breakup of the culture, it would eventually have happened, for somewhere along the line of technology there must be a breakdown point. Machines could only get so big. There had to be an end somewhere to complexity, be it in machines or living.

Decentralization may have helped a little, might have

hurried the process along by a thousand years or so, but that was all it amounted to.

And here once again Man had devised clever words—commonplace words—to dim the brightness of this frightening thing he could not understand. A teleporter was called a lifter; a telepath a tracer or a talker, the ability to follow worldliness a bit into the future was called second sight, while one who practiced it was usually called a peeker. And there were many other abilities, too—unrecognized or little better than half-guessed—all lumped under the general term of magic. But this did not matter greatly. A common and a homey word served just as well as correct terminology, and might even in the end lead to a readier acceptance. The thing that did matter greatly was that this time the abilities not be lost and not be pushed aside. Something would happen, something had to happen, to shock these people into a realization of what they really had.

So he went from camp to camp and now there was no need to ask the question, for the question went before him.

He went along the roads, a legend, and now he heard of another legend, a man who went from camp to camp dispensing medicines and cures.

It was only a rumor at first, heard oftener and oftener; finally he found a camp where the healer had stopped no more than a week before. Sitting around a campfire that evening, he listened to the wonder of the healer.

"Mrs. Cooper complained for years," an old crone told him. "Was sickly all the time. Kept to her bed for days. Couldn't keep nothing on her stomach. Then she took one bottle of this stuff and you should see her now. Sprightly as a jay."

Across the fire an old man nodded gravely. "I had rheumatiz," he said. "Just couldn't seem to shake it. Misery in my bones all the blessed time. The camp doc, he couldn't do a thing. Got a bottle of this stuff . . ."

He got up and danced a limber jig to put across his point.

In not one camp, but twenty, the story was the same—of those who left their beds and walked; of miseries disappeared; of complaints gone overnight.

Another one of them, Amby told himself. Another piece of magic. A man with the art of healing at his fingertips. Where would it end, he wondered.

Then he met the healer.

He came on the deserted camp after dusk had fallen. It was just at the hour when the suppers should be over, and the dishes done, and people would be gathering to sit around and talk. But there was not a soul around the trailers—except a dog or two at the garbage cans—and the streets that ran between the trailers echoed in their emptiness.

He stood in the center of the camp, wondering if he should shout to attract attention, but he was afraid to shout. Slowly he wheeled about, watching narrowly for the slightest motion, for the first pinprick of wrongness. It was then he saw the flare of light at the south edge of the camp.

Advancing cautiously toward it, he caught the murmur of the crowd when he was still a good ways off. He hesitated for a moment, doubtful if he should intrude, then went slowly forward.

The crowd, he saw, was gathered at the edge of a grove just beyond the camp. They were squeezed into a close-packed knot before a solitary trailer. The scene was lighted by a half dozen flares thrust into the ground.

A man stood on the steps that led to the trailer's door, and his voice floated faintly to where Amby stood; but faint as the words might be, there was a familiar pattern to them. Amby stood there, thinking back to boyhood, and a small town he had not thought of for years, and the sound of banjo music and the running in the streets. It had been exciting, he remembered, and they'd talked of it for days. Old Lady Adams, he remembered, had sworn by the medicine she'd bought, and waited patiently for years for the medicine show to come back to town again so she could get some more. But it never came again.

He walked forward to the edge of the crowd and a woman turned her head to tell him, whispering fiercely, "It's him!", as if it might be the Lord Almighty. Then she went back to listening.

The man on the steps was in full spiel by this time. He didn't talk so loud, but his voice carried and it had a quietness and a pompous, yet human, authority.

"My friends," he was saying. "I'm just an ordinary man. I wouldn't have you think different. I wouldn't want to fool you by saying I was somebody, because in fact I ain't. I don't even talk so good. I ain't much good at grammar. But maybe there are a lot of the rest of you who don't know much grammar, either, and I guess the most of you can understand me; so it'll be all right. I'd like to come right down there in the crowd and talk to each one of you, face to face, but you can hear me better if I stand up here. I'm not trying to put on any airs by standing up here on these steps. I ain't trying to put myself above you.

"Now I've told you that I wouldn't fool you, not even for a minute. I'd rather cut my tongue out and throw it to the hogs than tell you a thing that wasn't true. So I ain't going to make no high-flown claims for this medicine of mine. I'm going to start right out by being honest with you. I'm going to tell you that I ain't even a doctor. I never studied medicine. I don't know a thing about it. I just like to think of myself as a messenger—someone who is carrying good news.

"There's quite a story connected with this medicine and if you'll just hold still for a while I'd like to tell it to you. It goes a long ways back and some of it sounds almost unbelievable, but I wish you would believe me, for every word is true. First, I'll have to tell you about my old grandma. She's been dead these many years, God rest her. There never was a finer or a kinder woman and I remember when I was just a lad . . ."

Amby walked back from the crowd a ways and sat down limply on the ground.

The gall of the guy, he thought, the sheer impertinence!

When it was all over, when the last bottle had been sold, when the people had gone back to the camp and the medicine man was gathering up the flares, Amby rose and walked forward.

"Hello, Jake," he said.

13

Jake said, "Well, I tell you, Doc, I was kind of backed against the wall. We was down to nothing. No money for gasoline or grub and begging hadn't been so good. So I got to thinking, sort of desperate like. And I thought that just because a man's been honest all his life doesn't mean he has to keep on being honest. But for the life of me, I couldn't see how I could profit much even from dishonesty, except maybe stealing and that's too dangerous. Although I was ready to do most anything."

"I can believe that," Amby said.

"Aw, Doc," pleaded Jake, "What you keep pouring it on for? There ain't no sense of you staying sore. We was sorry right away we left you; we would have turned around right away and come back again, except that I was scared to. And, anyhow, it worked out all right."

He flipped the wheel a little to miss a rock lying in the road.

"Well, sir," he said, continuing with his story, "it does beat all how things will happen. Just when you figure you are sunk, something will turn up. We stopped along this river, you see, to try to catch some fish and the kids found an old dump there and got rooting around in it, the way kids will, you know. And they found a lot of bottles—four or five dozen of them—all of them alike. I imagine someone had hauled them out long ago and dumped them. I sat looking at those bottles, not having much of anything else to do, and I got to wondering if I had any use for them or if it would be just a waste of space hauling them along. Then all of a sudden it hit me just like that. They were all full of dirt and some of them were chipped, but we got them washed and polished up and . . ."

"Tell me, what did you put in the bottles?"

"Well, Doc, I tell you honest, I just don't remember what I used for that first batch."

135

"Nothing medicinal, I take it."

"Doc, I wouldn't have the slightest notion of what goes into medicine. The only thing to be careful of is not to put in anything that will kill them or make them very sick. But you got to make it unpleasant or they won't think it's any good. Myrt, she fussed some about it to start with, but she's all right now. Especially since people claim the stuff is doing them some good, although how in the world it could I can't rightly figure out. Doc, how in the world could stuff like that be any good at all?"

"It isn't."

"But folks claim it helps. There was this one old geezer . . ."

"It's conditioned faith," said Amby. "They're living in a world of magic and they're ready to accept almost anything. They practically beg for miracles."

"You mean it's all in their heads?"

"Every bit of it. These people have lost their sophistication, or you'd never got away with it; they'll accept a thing like that on faith. They drink the stuff and expect so confidently it will help them that it really does. They haven't been battered since they were old enough to notice with high-power advertising claims. They haven't been fooled time after time by product claims. They haven't been gypped and lied to and cajoled and threatened. So they're ready to believe."

"So that's the way it is," said Jake. "I'm glad to know; I worried some about it."

The kids were scuffling in the back seat and Jake chewed them out, but the kids went on scuffling. It was like old times again.

Amby settled back comfortably in the seat, watching the scenery go by. "You're sure you know where this camp is?"

"I can see it, Doc, just like it was yesterday. I remember it was funny those guys would need a rocket engineer."

He looked slantwise at Amby. "How come you're in such a lather to find this camp of theirs?"

"I got an idea," Amby told him.

"You know, Doc, I was thinking now that you're back

we might team up together. You with your white hair and that big lingo that you use ..."

"Forget it," Amby said.

"There ain't no harm in it," protested Jake. "We'd give them a show. That's what brought them out at first. It ain't like it used to be back before D. C., when there was television and the movies and baseball games and such. There ain't much entertainment now and they'd come out just to hear us talk."

Amby didn't answer.

It was good to be back again, he thought. He should be sore at Jake, but somehow he couldn't be. They'd all been so glad to see him—even the kids and Myrt— and they were trying so hard to make up for their deserting him.

And they'd do it all over again if the occasion ever arose where they thought it would be to their advantage; but in the meantime they were good people to be with, and they were heading where he'd wanted to go. He was satisfied. He wondered how long he would have had to hunt before he found the rocket camp if Jake had not turned up again. He wondered, vaguely, if he'd ever found it.

"You know," Jake said, "I been thinking it over and I might just run for congress. This medicine business has given me a lot of practice at public speaking and I know just the plank to run on—abolish this here road tax. I never heard anyone in all my life as burned up at anything as these folks are at the road tax."

"You couldn't run for congress," Amby told him. "You aren't a resident of any place. You don't belong to any camp."

"I never thought of that. Maybe I could join up with some camp long enough to ..."

"And you can't abolish the road tax if you want to keep the roads."

"Maybe you're right at that, Doc. But it does seem a shame these folks are pestered by the road tax. It sure has them upset."

He squinted at the dials on the instrument panel. "If we don't have any trouble," he said, "we'll be at that camp of yours by tomorrow evening."

14

They said, "It won't work." But that was one of the things he had known they'd say.

"It won't work if you don't co-operate," said Amby. "To do it you need fuel."

"We got fuel."

"Not good enough," said Amby; "not nearly good enough. This camp just down the road is working on some fuels."

"You want us to go down there with our hats in hand and . . ."

"Not with your hats in hand. You have something; they have something. Why don't you make a trade?"

They digested that, sitting in a circle under the big oak tree that grew in the center of the camp. He watched them digesting it—the hard and puzzled faces, the shrewd, nineteenth-century Yankee faces, the grease-grimed hands folded in their laps.

All around were the trailers with their windowboxes and their lines of washing, with the women-faces and the children-faces peering out of doors and windows, all being very silent; this was an important council, and they knew their place.

And beyond the trailers the great stacks of the farm machinery plant.

"I tell you, mister," said the business agent. "This rocket business is just a hobby with us. Some of the boys found some books about it and read up a little and got interested. And in a little while the whole camp got interested. We do it like some other camps play baseball or hold shooting matches. We aren't hell-for-leather set on doing something with it. We're just having fun."

"But if you could use the rockets?"

"We ain't prejudiced against using them, but we got to think it through."

"You would need some lifters."

"We've got lifters, mister; we got a lot of them. We pick up all we can. They cut down the operation costs, so we can afford to pay them what they ask. We use a lot of them in the assembly plant."

One of the younger men spoke up. "There's just one thing about it. Can a lifter lift himself?"

"Why couldn't he?"

"Well, you take a piece of pipe. You can pick it up without any trouble, say. But if you stand on it, you can tug your muscles out and you can't even budge it."

"A lifter can lift himself, all right," said the business agent. "We got one fellow in assembly who rides around at work—on the pieces he is lifting. Claims it's faster that way."

"Well, all right, then," said Amby. "Put your lifter in a trailer; he could lift it, couldn't he?"

The business agent nodded. "Easily."

"And handle it? Bring it down again without busting it all up?"

"Sure he could."

"But he couldn't move it far. How far would you say?"

"Five miles, maybe. Maybe even ten. It looks easy, sure, but there's a lot of work to it."

"But if you put rockets on the trailer, then all the lifter would have to do would be to keep it headed right. How hard would that be?"

"Well, I don't rightly know," the business agent said. "But I think it would be easy. He could keep it up all day."

"And if something happened? If a rocket burned out, say. He could bring it down to earth without smashing anything."

"I would say he could."

"What are we sitting here for, then?"

"Mister," asked the business agent, "what are you getting at?"

"Flying camps," said Amby "Can't you see it, man! Want to move somewhere else, or just go on vacation— why, the whole camp would take to the air and be there in no time."

The business agent rubbed his chin. "I don't say it wouldn't work," he admitted. "My guess is that it would. But why should we bother? If we want to go somewhere else we got all the time there is. We ain't in any hurry."

"Yes," said another man, "just tell us one good reason."

"Why, the road tax," Amby said. "If you didn't use the roads, you wouldn't have to pay the tax."

In the utter silence he looked around the circle, and he knew he had them hooked.

THE END

A new solution to the
puzzling problem of the UFO!

FLYING SAUCERS:
HOAX OR REALITY?

By L. Jerome Stanton

The author of this book is not a believer.
He is not a non-believer.
He is a scientifically trained writer with vast experience in this and related fields. He is unbiased, but exceedingly curious. He has sifted through the reports of the Air Force and the independent UFO research groups. By applying his own scientific knowledge, he has unearthed some **startling** facts never before disclosed!

This is by far the most informative book on the subject today.

Absorbing as a good mystery novel—but make no mistake —this is fact.

B50-761   50¢

FREE BOOKS!

Choose any 4 exciting Belmont Books listed below and receive the fifth book absolutely free! Choose 7 books and get 2 additional books free!